Joy

Merry ChristmaS

Learned
1254 S Shannon St Apt 208
Van Wert, OH 45891-2484

D1257925

A Fatal Yarn

Allie Pleiter

AnniesFiction.com

Books in the Secrets of the Castleton Manor Library series

. . . and more to come!

A Fatal Yarn
Copyright © 2018 Annie's.

All rights reserved. No part of this publication may be reproduced, stored in a
retrieval system, or transmitted in any form or by any means—electronic, mechanical,
photocopying, recording or otherwise—without the prior written permission of the
publisher. The only exception is brief quotations in printed reviews. For information
address Annie's, 306 East Parr Road, Berne, Indiana 46711-1138.

The characters and events in this book are fictional, and any resemblance to actual persons
or events is coincidental.

Library of Congress-in-Publication Data
A Fatal Yarn / by Allie Pleiter
p. cm.
I. Title
                        2018949182

AnniesFiction.com
(800) 282-6643
Secrets of the Castleton Manor Library™
Series Creator: Shari Lohner
Series Editor: Lorie Jones
Cover Illustrator: Jesse Reisch

10 11 12 13 14 | Printed in China | 9 8 7 6 5 4 3 2 1

Faith Newberry watched Watson's stumpy tail twitch.

Her black-and-white tuxedo cat was never short of his own opinions on the guests of Castleton Manor, the luxury retreat where they both lived.

The manor welcomed not only booklovers, authors, and other literary figures, but it famously extended its hospitality to pets as well. In fact, Faith always boasted that few places in the world embraced booklovers and their pets with more enthusiasm than Castleton Manor. Pets were just as pampered as any of the human guests. One of the delights of her job as librarian of the estate's spectacular private collection was Watson's ability to join her at work every day.

Watson's current curiosity did not surprise Faith one bit. As Watson looked out the leaded library windows of the French Renaissance château-style mansion, Faith wondered whether her cat was downright obsessed or highly irritated. The furious twitching of his tail and the laser-sharp focus of his green eyes told her that he was likely both.

Usually when Faith gazed out the windows, she marveled at the Victorian gardens, winding paths, fountains, topiaries, and other landscape features that lost little of their beauty even in the dead of a Cape Cod winter.

This morning, however, it was the pair of black sedans currently discharging their passengers onto the stately front drive that held their attention. The week's guest of honor—celebrity mystery author Dinah Harper—had arrived.

Watson had little reason to be impressed by the arrival of a celebrity author. Castleton, with its devotion to books and booklovers, had seen more than its fair share of events with well-known writers as the guests of honor. Nor was the cat drawn by the small knot of people who surrounded Dinah Harper in her vibrant peach-colored coat and dramatic silk scarf, striking as the woman was.

No, Watson's attention was firmly fixed on what Dinah held in her arms: a surprisingly large, outrageously fluffy rabbit. Faith had seen pictures of the bunny during her research for the upcoming Betty Townsend Week fan event, but in person, the animal was stunning.

"I told you this wasn't going to be a boring old Monday morning. That's Dinah Harper, best-selling author of the series of Betty Townsend mystery novels. But I don't think you're interested in Ms. Harper's success." She pointed at the animal Dinah held. "That, Rumpy, is Pouf, her Angora rabbit."

Watson, who'd never quite warmed to his nickname referencing his shortened tail, turned to Faith. The tilt of his head and the set of his eyes clearly said, "You're not serious."

Cats, dogs, and all number of animals regularly visited the manor, and they had more than once tested Watson's patience. The Betty Townsend Week conference set to begin this afternoon marked the first event to host a large number of long-eared guests.

"Yes, that really is a rabbit," Faith said. "And that very large, very fluffy one belongs to our distinguished guest. Which means that rabbit—and all the ones who will be following her later this afternoon—are off-limits. They are not toys. They are not adversaries." She gave her cat a serious look. "And they are most certainly not dinner."

Despite whatever ancient feline predatory instincts Watson might have harbored, Faith was relieved when Watson simply gave a low purr and stuck out his pink tongue as if to say, "Who'd want to eat that hair ball anyway?"

"There are going to be quite a lot of rabbits, so get used to it. A couple dozen will be staying in the manor when their bus arrives later today. After that, at least another dozen guests—and their rabbits—will be coming in for each day's events."

Faith hoped Watson's irritation was rising instead of his appetite. Annoyance with the creatures might help him keep his distance. But just in case he needed reminding, she pointed at him. "I expect you to rise to this challenge and behave yourself. That means no leaving the library without permission, no sudden appearances around the manor, no escaping the cottage when I leave you there, and no terrorizing bunnies."

Watson had proven quite skillful at all those things except terrorizing bunnies—thus far anyway. She hoped she wouldn't discover that he had any talents in that department. Still, a little bribery couldn't hurt. "There are a dozen tunaroons in it for you if you behave. Do we have a deal?"

She knew this wasn't quite fair. Her friend Midge Foster was Castleton's concierge veterinarian and the owner of Happy Tails Gourmet Bakery, and the tunaroons she sold there were Watson's weakness. However, it had the desired effect.

After seeming to give the proposal careful consideration, Watson pushed his black head against her arm.

Faith took that for the feline equivalent of a handshake and turned toward the library door. "Wolfe asked me to greet Ms. Harper and the others when they arrive, so I'll be back in a while. Consider this your first test. Stay here in the library and behave."

Remembering that Dinah Harper was almost as famous for her knitting as she was for her historical mystery novels and rabbits, Faith threw a lovely hand-knit shawl from her aunt Eileen Piper around her shoulders and headed down to meet the author.

"Dinah Harper and the two others from Baxter House Publishing are here," Marlene Russell, the manor's assistant manager, announced as she met Faith in the hallway.

"I saw them from the library window," Faith shared, quickening her pace to match Marlene's usual brisk efficiency. "I have to say, Pouf is much bigger than I thought she would be."

"Pouf?" Marlene wrinkled her nose. "Oh, you mean the rodent."
She had never been a fan of the manor's pet-friendly policies, and
Faith suspected the incoming herd of rabbits pushed all her buttons.
Marlene jingled the large ring of keys that never left her waist—a clear
sign of her anxiety and annoyance.

Forget the tunaroons, Faith thought. It might serve everyone better
to ensure that a continual flow of cookies and other baked goods made
it to Marlene's desk every morning this week. The bulk of the rabbits
and guests hadn't even arrived yet, and Marlene already seemed strung
as tight as a drum.

"Dinah Harper and her fans are famous for the love they show
their rabbits," Faith advised, hoping to smooth things over for this
first meeting. "It probably wouldn't be wise to use the word *rodent*
around them."

Consummate professional that she was, Marlene would likely
never let any guest see her true feelings for the rabbits. The woman's
grimace, however, confirmed to Faith that the incoming animal
guests were about to tax Marlene's natural reactions just as much as
Watson's—if not more.

Marlene paused her walking, took in a deep, unsteady breath,
and turned to Faith, cringing. "I've read up on the little beasts. They
nibble on everything. Wires, furniture, fabrics, even books. How can
you of all people be calm about this?"

"Because we will be fine," came a deep, reassuring voice from
behind them.

Faith and Marlene spun to face Wolfe Jaxon, co-owner of the
manor. He was exactly the kind of person one would expect to run a
beautiful, high-end resort: tall and handsome, with dark hair flecked
with dignified gray, bright-blue eyes, and a charismatic smile. While
his family had always owned the estate, Wolfe's mother, Charlotte, had
been the one to repurpose the huge nineteenth-century family home
as a vacation and retreat spot over ten years before.

"Our pet owners have overwhelmingly been responsible, respectful people," Wolfe continued. "I know Dinah Harper and her staff have made some unusual requests of us for this week, but I don't think these rabbit fans will be any different. So let's treat them well."

Marlene gave an equally large exhale. "I'll try." For all her fussing and irritability, Marlene always did whatever was required of her. "But if so much as one drapery tassel ends up a bunny snack—"

"We'll handle it," Wolfe said. He pushed open the vestibule's large entrance doors, allowing three people and one rabbit to make their way up into the entranceway. He smiled at the newcomers. "Welcome to Castleton Manor."

"It's spectacular," Dinah marveled, shifting the huge white rabbit to one arm as she extended the other to shake Wolfe's hand. "The perfect setting for Betty Townsend Week. The fans will adore it."

Wolfe gestured to Faith. "May I introduce Faith Newberry, librarian of the manor's private collection? Which, I'm delighted to say, now includes several first editions of your books that I hope you'll do the honor of signing for us."

Wolfe's classic good looks were only outdone by his charming personality. Faith was grateful they had an easy friendship, but she was never unaware of all the reasons Wolfe was Lighthouse Bay's most eligible bachelor.

"Copies of all seventeen of your Betty Townsend mysteries have arrived for the public charity book sale later this week," Faith offered. "Although I expect all the manor guests already own multiple copies."

"I hope the fans and the public buy lots of books anyway," Dinah said. "With Easter two months away, the Rabbit Rescue League can use all the funds we can raise." She regarded her pet. "A bunny is a responsibility never to be taken lightly. Isn't that right, Pouf?"

"She's beautiful," Faith said. The compliment was genuine. Up close, the rabbit's long, snow-white coat really was impressive, even if she knew Watson would never share that opinion. "May I?"

"Absolutely." Dinah plopped the rabbit right into Faith's arms. "Pouf loves to meet new people. She's a regular Angora ambassador in my opinion."

Faith hid her surprise. She had just meant to pet the animal.

"I'll have your luggage delivered upstairs, but does Miss Pouf have a bed, cage, or habitat of some sort you need us to set up?" Marlene asked Dinah.

It was likely only Wolfe and Faith could hear the carefully concealed anxiety in Marlene's question.

Wolfe, suave as ever, stepped in to assist without missing a beat. "This is Ms. Marlene Russell, our assistant manager. She'll be masterful at handling the logistics for your event, Ms. Harper."

"Call me Dinah, please. Pouf's hutch goes in my room. It's in the sedan with my luggage and such." She turned to a smartly dressed young woman with sleek black hair to her left. "You sent them all those details, didn't you, Maura?"

The young woman extended a hand to Marlene. "Maura Webber, Dinah's editor and publicist."

"Yes, we've spoken many times on the phone," Marlene replied. Her usual tone when dealing with guests—a combination of professional competence and welcome that always inspired trust—was firmly back in place. "And you must be Mr. Powers?"

A man in a dark suit and a dramatic blue tie behind Maura glanced up from his cell phone. "Ron Powers, CEO of Baxter House Publishing."

"Baxter House has been my publisher since day one," Dinah said fondly as she reclaimed Pouf from Faith. "Ron's father was my first editor, so I guess that makes me a family heirloom. There'd be no Betty Townsend without Baxter House."

Ron smiled. "I think you deserve the credit for putting Betty Townsend on the cultural map."

"Don't be modest. Betty would still be just a figment of my

imagination without you and the other lovely people at Baxter House," Dinah said grandly. She beamed at Faith, Wolfe, and Marlene. "Now you've met the team. I'll let you all handle the details while Pouf and I check out our lodgings."

"You will be staying in the beautiful Daphne du Maurier Suite," Marlene informed her. "It features large east-facing windows with gorgeous views of both the woods and the sea."

"What's not to love about that?" Dinah said. "It's been a long drive up from New York, and I'd like to enjoy a bit of peace and quiet staring out those windows before all the excitement starts."

"Twenty-four overnight guests and another dozen day attendees, correct?" Marlene consulted her file. "And twenty-two rabbits," she added with a barely noticeable wrinkle of her nose.

"Oh, it'll end up being more than that," Dinah assured her. "The day guests will bring their rabbits, and the rabbit show should attract even more. I wouldn't be surprised if fans bring their bunnies to the public signing too."

Faith heard Marlene pull in a tight breath.

"Ms. Russell," Maura said, "why don't you and I meet later this afternoon and go over all those details? I'm sure we'd both like to have everything in place before the bus with the overnight guests arrives. For now, I'd like to see the library and talk to Faith."

"Of course." If Marlene was irritated at her agenda being placed second behind the library—and Faith was sure she was—she hid her annoyance behind an efficient smile. "I'll expect you shortly. Perhaps Mr. Powers and I can go over some details while you sightsee?"

As Marlene and Ron marched off at her usual brisk pace and Wolfe escorted Dinah to her suite, Faith led Maura down the hallway in the direction of the library.

"I saw the brochure and the website," Maura said. "Floor-to-ceiling bookshelves and all that woodwork. It sounds like a fabulous vibe. Actually, that's why I want to talk to you and see it."

While "vibe" was an odd way of putting it, Faith had to agree. "It really is a lovely space."

"Wow," Maura marveled as Faith unlocked the library doors and led the editor inside. "The photos don't even come close to doing it justice."

Faith smiled. Watching booklovers take in the splendor of the library never got old. Cozy groupings of tufted chairs in regal red upholstery begged for a curl-up with a good book. Huge red-curtained windows let in a generous wash of sunlight by day, and ornate standing lamps lit the room by night. Even the painted ceilings added to the room's opulent feel.

For all the architectural elegance, it was the collection inside the space that impressed most guests.

"As work environments go, it's pretty amazing," Faith said, gesturing toward the vaulted shelves. "Mr. Jaxon has a first-rate private collection as well, but the array of rare volumes in here is among the finest I've ever seen."

Maura glanced around the room. "This whole setup is the perfect place to gather Dinah's fans. I can't believe Claudia never suggested booking Betty Townsend Week here before. Ron hadn't even heard of the place before I brought it up."

"Claudia?"

Maura appeared irritated. "Claudia Ferguson, the old editor they let go to hire me." She didn't say "old" with any amount of respect. "Clearly, they needed someone with better instincts to get Dinah back to the top of the best-seller lists."

"Well, we don't promote Castleton Manor very much. We don't have to. I'm sure Marlene told you that we're usually booked way in advance. It's quite a stroke of luck that a cancellation enabled you to get this slot when you did."

"You only get what you go for, I always say." Maura gazed up at the library's tall stacks, gasping when she noticed the ornate balcony that gave the library additional drama.

From his perch on the windowsill, Watson gave a loud meow, as if to say, "I'm splendid too, aren't I?"

Maura turned at the sound. "Look at you!" she said with a grin. "Every good stock of books needs a resident cat, doesn't it?"

"I'd certainly agree with that. Although Watson belongs to me rather than to the manor." Faith smiled. "But as you can tell, no one has been able to convince him that he doesn't own the place."

Maura laughed. "I have to say, I think the pet gimmick is a great one. It's clever marketing, and it works really well for us."

Faith wasn't sure *gimmick* was the word Wolfe or his mother would use to describe the manor's pet-friendly policies. "I like to think we understand how important animals can be to our guests. Their pets are like family, and they should be able to travel like family. I definitely love that I get to bring Watson to work with me."

"That is quite a perk," Maura said.

Faith walked to her desk. "I want you to know that I plan for Watson to be keeping to himself at home for the entire week. I suspect the incoming rabbit population might prove a bit much for him."

Maura nodded as Watson consented to let her stroke his gleaming black-and-white coat. "I can imagine. I agree with you on that, Watson. The bunnies are a bit much. Pouf is only the beginning. Just you wait and see." She turned to Faith. "In any case, I'm delighted we got this venue. This is a critical event for Dinah. And for me."

Faith sat down and motioned for Maura to sit in the guest chair beside her desk. None of this explained why the editor needed to see the library before coordinating all the other event details. "Please tell me how I can help you."

"Like I said, I'm here to turn things around. Orchestrate a major shift in Dinah's career," Maura explained as she sat. "Dinah believes it's important for the fans to like me. She's viewing the event as an introduction of sorts—me to the fans. I don't usually concern myself with such things, but Dinah thinks that getting to know me will help them swallow the shift more easily."

"What shift is that?"

"Have you read any of Dinah's novels?"

Slightly taken aback by the apparent change of subject, Faith picked up the copy of *Betty Townsend and the Morse Code Murder* that Eileen had lent her for the book club to which they both belonged. "I'd intended to dig into her latest this evening. But my aunt is a big fan."

"*Morse Code Murder* presents an evolution in style for Dinah. We're moving her away from the small frontier town setting and into more exciting World War I intrigue. You know, something to bring in a younger crowd. Fast-paced plots, foreign locales, a bit of glamour, and naturally a heavy dose of romance. Nothing too steamy, but it definitely sizzles."

"I see." Faith remembered Eileen saying she wasn't as fond of this new book as she had been of Dinah's numerous other novels, but she kept that opinion to herself.

Maura pointed at the book's stylish cover. "Ron and I have had a bit of a challenge convincing Dinah that she'll need to make a few changes to stay relevant. It's a new market. She's got to appeal to younger fans."

"Are these younger fans coming this week?"

Maura tucked her sleek hair behind an ear. "Not as many as I'd like, but that will change. Dinah's a smart woman. She's coming around to our way of thinking. This week is mostly about coddling her die-hard fans. Getting the 'bunny crowd,' if you will, to come on board. A new crop of readers will boost Dinah's drooping sales, but we're going to have to make nice with her loyal fans too."

It seemed like a tall order, but it still didn't explain what the library had to do with achieving that goal. Faith folded her hands on the desk. "It sounds like you've got your work cut out for you this week."

"Exactly. Which is why I need private access to the library for my early morning yoga practice. It's crucial to keeping my focus."

"The manor has several private places, not to mention a gym and even a yoga room. Why do you want to do yoga in the library?"

"People can find me in my room, in the gym, or outside. I need someplace unexpected, somewhere no one would think to look. That's here. The vibe is exactly what I was hoping for. I don't want anyone to know where I am except for you. I'll need to be absolutely certain I won't be disturbed."

"But our guests might want—"

"At five in the morning? I doubt it. So you can give me a key and I can just let myself in, right?"

Faith knew Dinah and her publishing house had paid a premium price to book the manor on short notice. They were prime customers. Still, it was not her call to give a guest a library key. "We want to accommodate you, but this is a highly unusual request."

Maura raised one dark eyebrow. "I was told you had authority to place anything from the library at our disposal."

"I'll still need to get a request like this cleared with Ms. Russell."

Maura frowned. "We're going to have some serious chaos here. You wouldn't want anything to happen to Dinah because I lost focus, would you?" Something about the editor's tone left a chill in the air.

Faith gulped. Was Maura being dramatic, or was there really some kind of threat descending on the manor?

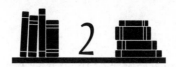

2

An hour later, Dinah sat in the library, talking with Faith and Maura as she signed special editions of *Betty Townsend and the Morse Code Murder* to be given to the event attendees.

They chatted amiably until the subject of Dinah's fans came up. Then the mood turned a bit chilly.

"Your loyal fans need to forget about the past and embrace the future," Maura said.

Dinah waved dismissively. "Really, you've got to stop talking that way about my Bettys."

"Bettys?" Faith asked.

"That's what Dinah's fans call themselves," Maura explained, rolling her eyes.

"Do you feel there's any dissension among your fans about the new direction?" Faith asked the author.

"Of course there is," Dinah answered. "The Bettys are my most loyal fans. How could they not have strong opinions about what Betty does? But I think Maura's overdramatizing the situation."

Maura's lips tightened, but she didn't say anything.

"I've always found the Bettys to be one of the best parts of my career," Dinah continued as she picked up the next book and added her large, sweeping signature. "They attend my events, send me e-mails like there's no tomorrow, and even write me good old-fashioned snail mail. They're wonderful at giving feedback."

"They are vocal—I'll give them that." Maura clearly considered that a mixed blessing.

"And generous," Dinah added. "They've given loads of money to the Rabbit Rescue League. Most of them own rabbits, just like Betty.

They're also very loyal. Some of them have been with me from the first book."

Maura opened another box of books. "But many of them aren't fond of change. Even good change."

"Yes, there have been a few jitters with the new direction," Dinah admitted. "But there were jitters when I had Betty cut her hair."

"I'd qualify this as a bit more than jitters," Maura argued. Then she addressed Faith. "I've told Dinah I think there's a genuine conflict brewing. One that may come to a head this week."

Faith felt a twinge of anxiety. Betty Townsend Week was supposed to be a delightful gathering of a mystery-solving fictional telephone operator's fans. If Maura was to be believed, the event would be more of a showdown of clashing opinions about Betty's adventures. Maybe Marlene—and the rest of the staff, Faith included—had more to worry about than just bunnies.

"Now stop that," Dinah scolded. "I keep telling you there's absolutely nothing to worry about. Every Betty and her rabbit will be perfect guests from the moment they arrive."

Maura gave her a skeptical look.

"My Bettys can have differences of opinions without their discussions escalating into fights," Dinah said. "Besides, I've already spoken to Francine about all this, and she's pledged to help us keep the peace if anything flares up."

"You've spoken to Francine?" Maura sounded surprised.

Dinah nodded as she reached for the next book. "You'll like Francine Nelson," she said to Faith. "A great lover of books and rabbits. Francine's the president of the Bettys and the owner of an absolutely outstanding Angora."

Out of the corner of her eye, Faith caught Watson's movement in the library window.

With all this talk of rabbits, his stubby tail constantly twitched in what she imagined was suspicion of the incoming long-eared guests.

The Angora avalanche descending on the manor might very well be too much, even for a cat of his extraordinary disposition. She was amazed that he hadn't already pulled one of his famous disappearing acts.

"I think I'm right to be concerned," Maura said. "Francine holds a lot of sway with the Bettys but only with the older ones. The younger ones have opinions of their own, and they're not afraid to express them. I think there's only so much Francine can do to keep the peace if things get out of hand."

"My fans are passionate, not dangerous," Dinah insisted. "There's a difference."

"Well, no one can say they aren't vocal in their opinions of late," Maura said with a weary tone.

Dinah huffed and put down her pen. "Well, yes, I know a few have groused long and hard about the shift—"

"Too many," Maura interjected.

"But I try to be thankful that Betty is so dear to them that they care enough to grouse. Young people love change. They thrive on it. But for the rest of us, change is difficult and a little scary."

"Change is necessary," Maura asserted.

Faith got the distinct impression they were no longer discussing just Betty's fans but possibly her creator too.

"That doesn't mean it isn't challenging," Dinah replied. "Goodness, Betty is my own brainchild, and even I had a hard time getting behind the shift at first."

"But you got behind it, and it's working," Maura pointed out.

"The Bettys will get behind it too if we give them time. That's why this week is so important. It reminds us all of what we have in common, what we love about Betty and our rabbits."

The expression on the editor's face clearly said she didn't agree, but she was evidently tired of the argument—at least for the moment.

Dinah returned to signing. "Don't worry. This is your first Betty Townsend Week. I know you think you need to protect me, but by the end of the event, if not the end of the first day, you'll see what a great community the Bettys can be."

Maura sighed. "I hope so."

"You just watch," Dinah said. "Once the rabbit and knitting competitions get under way, everyone will be too busy to even think about being upset."

Maura had explained the exhibitions and competitions that went along with Betty Townsend Week, but Faith still wasn't sure she understood the whole business. The rabbits were showcased and judged, apparently much like a dog or a horse show. Only this event also had a second show: an angora yarn knitting competition. Something about garments or accessories made from knitting up the hair of the bunnies? No doubt about it—this was going to be an interesting week.

Dinah leaned toward Faith. "Francine Nelson, the president I mentioned earlier? Her champion Angora, Beatrice, has won the competition each of the last four years. I doubt this year will be any different. She's also a masterful knitter. So you can understand why she's so highly respected among the Bettys."

Faith thought she caught an expression on Maura's face that didn't quite agree with that assessment. "If there are tensions between the fans, wouldn't a competition just make things worse? And how can you be so sure Beatrice will win the competition?" Faith asked, feeling ridiculous for even phrasing such a question. "You, Maura, and Ron judge the competition fairly, don't you?"

"Well, of course we do, my dear," Dinah replied. "But oh, my goodness, wait until you see Beatrice. She's an absolutely magnificent bunny." She held her hands apart, indicating a size Faith could hardly imagine for something called a "bunny."

Even Watson appeared a little shocked, and Faith made a mental note to be sure the feline was safely ensconced in their cottage before the rest of the rabbits arrived. She didn't want to see what would happen to his self-esteem if he met a rabbit that was large enough to turn him from predator to prey.

"Do you have any idea why the shift has made some fans so upset?" Faith asked. "Does it go beyond wanting your books to stay the way they've been?"

"I don't think so." Dinah finished another signature with a flourish. "They simply want to keep the old familiar Betty, and I'll continue to give her to them."

"Just in some exciting new settings," Maura added as she closed another box of signed books.

"I do think Maura and Ron are right. Betty needs new adventures. I find the young new fans energizing." Dinah smiled. "Maura has wonderful ideas. Did you know my Pouf has a social media account now? Who'd have imagined?"

"@PoufBookBunny," Maura said. "She reports behind-the-scenes info for the die-hard fans and gets them involved by asking how they liked the latest book. There are also polls about who's new to Betty and how they like the older books versus the new one. That has gotten us some invaluable information, I can tell you. The account has five thousand followers already. I've got a hashtag set up for the event too." The editor held up her phone to show what Faith could only describe as the first bunny glamour shot she'd ever seen.

"She's one busy bunny," Faith commented. She glanced over to see if Watson was peering at the dolled-up photo of the rabbit on a plush satin pillow. He might enjoy that level of pampering and public attention. After all, Faith had often joked with her friend Brooke Milner—the manor's head chef—that Watson thought he actually ran the manor.

"That's my Pouf." Dinah laughed. "The official Betty spokes-bunny."

"Don't you think Watson could be Castleton Manor's spokes-cat?" Maura asked, walking over to show Watson the photo on her phone. "We could set you up as @CastletonCat in no time, Watson. What do you think of that?"

Faith was relieved to see Watson take one look at the photo and turn back toward the window as if he found the suggestion ridiculous. His stumpy tail began to twitch, telling Faith he'd seen something through the window that interested him far more than promotional stunts.

Thus, it didn't surprise Faith when Marlene poked her head through the library door and announced, "Our bus of guests just arrived. Two hours early."

"I'm so excited!" Dinah said, jumping out of her chair to rush toward the window. "The Bettys are here!"

"So early?" Faith asked.

"Those are my Bettys—full of enthusiasm and surprises." Dinah started gathering her things. "I'd best get upstairs, so Pouf and I can get ready to meet them."

"Marlene, did you get my text?" Faith asked.

"About the key for Miss Webber? Yes, and that will be fine. I was coming to tell you when I saw the bus arrive. In fact, while I'm thinking about it, I might as well hand it over now." Marlene pulled a key from her ring and handed it to Maura, who had joined her at the doorway.

"Thank you," Maura said. "My days just aren't the same without my morning yoga."

"If there's anything else we can do for you, please don't hesitate to let us know." Marlene was out the door almost before she finished speaking.

Maura pocketed the key and smiled at Dinah. "Take your time. I'll grab Ron, and we'll chat with the Bettys so you can make a grand entrance." She waved and followed Marlene out.

"Maura's a bit driven, I know," Dinah told Faith. "But I have to say, she's marvelously efficient. I've gotten more done with Maura than I ever did with my previous editor. I'd never have guessed that such a fast pace would agree with me."

"I'm glad it's working out so well," Faith said.

Dinah glanced at the stack of remaining books. "Can you have the rest of these sent up to my room? I'll finish the signatures before I get dressed for tonight's opening dinner."

"Certainly," Faith agreed. "But first, I think our 'spokes-cat' needs to be off the premises so he doesn't alarm your guests." She pointed to Watson's current highly focused crouch at the window.

"Oh, he looks like a perfect gentleman. Right down to the tuxedo."

Watson's black-and-white coloring had made more than one guest comment about his built-in formal wear.

"Watson is many things," Faith said as she scooped up the feline, who gave an indignant yowl, "but he is still a cat. I'd prefer to be on the safe side until he can get his bearings amid all those bunnies."

If that's even possible, she thought.

The cat had become a prisoner in his own home. He stared out at the manor from his cottage window, the sting of his exile still fresh in his whiskers. Spokes-cat, indeed.

It was all because of the rabbits. There seemed to be dozens of them. They came in more shapes and sizes than the treats at that lovely place where his human got his tunaroons.

Their owners had set up collections of wire pens all over the lawn between his cottage and the manor, and now the absurd creatures were hopping about, likely nibbling what was left of the fine turf down to the roots. The thought of them wandering around his manor, while he was required to stay away, was enough to set his fur on edge.

They resembled nervous little sheep, leaping and munching and generally acting silly. He didn't want to consider what they would do to the guest rooms. He dreaded the thought of them roaming the hallways. He shuddered at the vision of them frolicking about in his favorite room.

Surely his human wouldn't be foolish enough to let those nibbling monsters into the library. Would she?

Worst of all, his human seemed to actually find the furry things fascinating. His own properly proportioned ears flattened at the sight of those outrageously long ears, those odd little noses that never stopped twitching, and all that hair. It shocked him that any sensible human could love a giant, hopping hair ball.

The cat was sure that nothing good would come of this new breed of manor guest. Something was a-paw, and there was no lucky rabbit to be had here this week.

He knew what his human had said: "Stay here." And it wasn't as if he wanted to go wandering among the dozens of fluffy invaders. But a cat's duty was a cat's duty, and if that meant tangling with the herd of long-eared beasts to investigate possible threats, then at least no one could call him a coward.

Sneaky perhaps. Stealthy, more accurately. But never cowardly.

When Faith returned from depositing a clearly displeased Watson in the old gardener's cottage that served as her residence, she found the manor overrun with readers and rabbits.

The Monday afternoon was unseasonably warm and sunny for February, but Faith was still surprised to see the collection of fenced-in circular wire pens that had already been erected on the side lawn. Each pen held a small group of rabbits wandering happily inside. Around the corrals, groups of Bettys stood chatting like mothers at a playground.

The diversity of rabbits was astounding—large and small, black, white, brown, and many colors in between. Faith felt like she'd stepped into a rabbit zoo.

Walking up to one pen, she bent down to peer at an enormous

mound of white-and-brown fur. "He's stunning," she remarked to the owner, a short, round woman with a severe bun of snow-white hair and cool gray eyes. "I had no idea they came that large with quite so much fur. How do you keep his white coat so clean?"

"*She* is always perfectly clean. I spend a lot of time ensuring that, and rabbits self-groom as well." For a woman with a rounded face, she had a decidedly pointed nose over which she scowled at Faith.

As if eager to put some distance between herself and this riffraff who didn't know she was female, the bunny hopped to the other side of the pen.

Faith dearly hoped she hadn't just insulted Francine Nelson and Beatrice. "I'm terribly sorry. What's her name?"

"Lady Latte," the woman said, pronouncing the name with great importance. "She's won three state titles."

"I can imagine." Faith held out her hand and offered her friendliest of smiles. "I'm Faith Newberry, the librarian here at Castleton Manor."

That seemed to score points with the woman. "Oh, that's why I didn't recognize you. I confess I thought you were one of those." She waved a dismissive hand toward another pen.

Faith glanced over and noticed the group had clearly divided itself between the multiple pens of older fans and their rabbits and one or two pens of younger guests and their animals.

As much as it felt nice to be classified as "younger," the disdain in the woman's voice let Faith know being "one of those" was definitely not a compliment. Maybe Maura's assessment of the conflict—and her resulting need for highly private yoga—wasn't so far-fetched after all. The frosty attitude coming off the woman called for half a dozen angora sweaters.

A guest is a guest, and all are welcome, Faith reminded herself. "Welcome to Castleton Manor. And you are?"

"Mrs. Pearl Quinton. Vice president of the Betty Townsend Fan Club."

It spoke volumes that she had used the club's formal name, not the "Bettys" nickname.

"It's a pleasure to meet you, Mrs. Quinton. And the beautiful Lady Latte here." Given the size and fur of this animal, Faith looked forward to seeing how much bigger and fluffier Francine Nelson's champion rabbit must be. "Could you perhaps point out Mrs. Nelson to me? I'd like to introduce myself to her as well."

Pearl pointed across the lawn. "Two pens over, beyond the upstarts and their beasts."

"You don't mean the younger Bettys?"

Pearl clearly didn't take to the idea of sharing the mantle of "Betty" with Dinah's younger fans. She frowned in the direction of the fans in question. "They show up out of nowhere with their digital this and their digital that, acting like they're the first people to discover Angoras and knitting and books. I'm not for it. Not at all."

"But surely they love the books and the rabbits just as much as you do," Faith said. "You've got that in common."

Pearl sniffed again. "I don't have anything in common with those young hooligans. Look at the way they're dressed. They have no respect for an estate like this and literature in general. Why, I'd wager they dog-ear pages and write in the margins. That's if they bother with paper books at all."

Goodness, Faith thought. Maura hadn't exaggerated. Passions clearly ran high among Betty Townsend fans. "Thank you for pointing out Mrs. Nelson," Faith said, eager to have this tense conversation over with. "I hope you enjoy your stay." With that attitude, Faith wasn't sure how an enjoyable stay was possible for the likes of Pearl Quinton.

"Mind your back with those young impostors, Miss Newberry," Pearl said as Faith made her way in the direction Pearl had indicated. "They're here to make trouble. I guarantee it."

3

After that pronouncement, Faith decided to make a point of stopping at the rabbit pen surrounded by younger fans.

One woman in a beautifully knit pink hat with the words *Boston Bettys* worked into the headband excitedly held up her phone. "She followed me back!" the woman boasted to her companions. "Pouf replied to my message and followed me back!"

"Pouf is a most gracious rabbit," Faith said, thinking she much preferred the young woman's enthusiasm to Pearl's judgmental nature. "Have you met her yet?"

"Not yet," the woman said. She appeared to be in her late twenties with wide brown eyes sparkling out through wire eyeglasses. "Have you?"

"It so happens that Ms. Harper introduced me to Pouf just this morning."

"So you've met her? Dinah? She's here already?" The group lit up with questions and exclamations.

Faith hoped Pearl Quinton was close enough to hear. These women seemed just as worthy of the Betty name as the older woman ready to deny them membership.

"She and Pouf seem very nice," Faith told the group. "I know she's excited to meet her newer fans like yourself. She told me as much."

"Not as excited as we are to meet her," another young woman in a brightly striped cowl-necked sweater said. "After I read her latest, I downloaded every Betty book I could find and whizzed through them as fast as I could. And I got a rabbit. That little brown guy is mine." She pointed to a small chocolate-brown bunny hopping about the pen.

"I don't have a rabbit yet," the woman in the pink hat said. "But I've always loved knitting, and I've loved the books from the beginning." She smiled at the rabbits in the pen. "They're amazing, aren't they?"

"They're lovely," Faith replied. "I'm already learning so much about Angora rabbits. I'm Faith Newberry, the librarian here at Castleton Manor."

"They have their own librarian here?" a third woman asked. "What a fabulous job."

Faith returned her wide smile. "I think so."

"It'd be like being on vacation all the time," the first woman said.

"It really is. I never get tired of being here. It might have a few tough spots, as all jobs do," she said, thinking of Marlene's never-ending list of demands. "But it's absolutely a dream post."

Working here had indeed come with dozens of challenges and quite a few frightening moments since she began her tenure. If a building could have a talent, Castleton's was to attract mystery and adventure as well as booklovers and their pets.

"I'm Annette Higgins," the owner of the pink hat said. "I'm the only one attending from Boston. Everyone else around this pen is from the New Jersey fan club."

A chorus of hellos and introductions greeted Faith.

Dinah was right. Her newest fans did have an infectious energy and seemed a very friendly bunch. But Maura was also right. The older fans weren't welcoming of the younger ones. Maybe by the end of the week, Dinah really would succeed in bringing them all together and boosting her career. This event surely seemed like the ideal place to remind the Bettys of everything they had in common—and they seemed to have a great deal in common, from the books, hats, mittens, sweaters, and rabbits Faith had already seen.

"I hope you enjoy your stay at the manor and your time with Dinah," Faith said as she walked on.

"We will," several of the young Bettys replied cheerfully.

Faith thought Pearl should rethink her assumptions about these friendly newcomers. But she reminded herself it wasn't her role to make peace among the Bettys. Instead, she focused on welcoming the guests. Faith approached a tall, graceful woman surrounded by a group of fans.

Francine Nelson looked every inch the president of the Betty Townsend Fan Club. Fine-featured with an upsweep of darker silver hair, Francine wore a beautiful cable-knit cardigan sweater in fuzzy sky-blue angora. The silk scarf around her neck reminded Faith of the way Dinah had worn her scarf. The woman had a commanding presence that would have impressed even Watson. She stood amid the lively discussion taking place among the women as regally as if she were holding court.

"Lieutenant Drake isn't as good a match as Sheriff Gardner was. Not even close," one woman said, shaking her head. "I can't help thinking that Drake is too slick for the likes of our Betty."

"Drake has shown himself to be an honorable man." Francine crossed her arms over her chest. "But I agree, Gardner still wins my vote." She had the tone of a mother choosing among suitors for a precious daughter. Given Francine's and the other fans' devotion to the young and single Betty, perhaps the comparison wasn't that far off.

As Faith stepped into the circle, Francine turned to Faith and asked, "What do you think?"

Faith gulped at the question. "I'm afraid I haven't read the books yet."

Francine raised an eyebrow. "Well, why in heaven's name are you here?"

"I work here. I'm the manor's librarian. Dinah's told me so much about you and the Bettys that I wanted to introduce myself." Faith held out her hand. "I'm Faith Newberry, and we're delighted to be hosting you at Castleton Manor." She nodded toward the pen. "You and all your amazing rabbits."

Francine broke into a warm smile. "A librarian who hasn't read a Betty Townsend novel?" She glanced around the group. "We'll certainly have to change that, won't we, ladies?"

A chorus of agreement went up among the women.

Noticing Faith's wrap, Francine's smile widened. "Do you knit, Miss Newberry?"

"Please call me Faith. And I don't, but my aunt Eileen does. She made this. Now, she's a librarian who knows quite a lot about Betty Townsend novels. She's a big fan of Dinah's books, and she's the librarian at our town library."

"Wonderful. You must invite her to join us at the show or the signing," Francine insisted. "Any friend of Betty's is a friend of ours."

As if to cast doubt on that declaration, one of Francine's companions cast a disparaging look toward the group Faith had just left. "Well, most of them, anyway."

A few others joined in her mumbling disapproval.

"Now, Gretchen," Francine said, raising a quieting hand. "I told you Dinah's asked us to do our best to be gracious to the young people. After all, I see quite a few splendid bunnies over there."

"I certainly see a few right here," Faith said. She gestured to the largest, fluffiest, most impressive rabbit in the pen. "Is this the renowned Beatrice?"

Dinah hadn't overstated the animal. She really was magnificent. While it was true Faith couldn't say how much of the mass was fur and how much of it was the actual animal somewhere inside the giant white ball of fluff, Beatrice appeared three times Watson's size.

Francine puffed up with pride. "It most certainly is. My champion girl."

"Back to defend her title," Gretchen added. "My Sterling never stands a chance. Not that I'm here to win."

"Don't be so modest," Francine said, placing a hand on Gretchen's arm. "You've taken more than your share of ribbons in the knitting competition. And Sterling is a delightful bunny." She gestured to a beautiful silvery-gray rabbit. "Look at that color," she said, addressing Faith. "It just mesmerizes, don't you think?"

Faith had never seen such a display of fluffy rabbit diversity. "I really am amazed by it all. Betty Townsend Week is going to be one of the most memorable events this year."

Francine nodded. "I have to say I agree with you there. I think Dinah is right when she says this gathering will be a pivotal moment in Betty Townsend history. Won't it, ladies?"

"Absolutely!" came the cries of agreement.

Faith spent the rest of the afternoon either getting work done or giving quick tours of the library to curious Bettys.

About an hour before she was scheduled to leave, she found the stack of *Betty Townsend and the Morse Code Murder* copies Dinah had left behind. She had completely forgotten to have them taken to Dinah's room as she had requested. Faith packed the half a dozen books into a box she had on hand and headed in the direction of the Daphne du Maurier Suite, where Dinah was staying.

"I can't believe you!" An emotional female voice from the stairwell startled Faith as she passed.

"Stop yelling. Do you want everyone to hear us?" snapped an equally upset male voice.

"Maybe they should," the female voice replied. "Maybe then I'd know if you really had something to hide."

The accusation stopped Faith in her tracks.

"Maura, I said I'm taking care of it. It's nothing you need to worry about. Why won't you believe me?"

Faith backed up against the wall. It was Maura, and she was arguing with Ron. Only their voices didn't sound very much like a professional argument.

"Maura, honey—"

Faith nearly dropped the box she was holding.

"Don't you 'Maura honey' me. Whatever else we were—"

"Were?" Ron sounded shocked and hurt.

Exactly what kind of argument was Faith hearing?

"I can't say because I'm Dinah's editor and I don't know what's going on here," Maura said. Then it sounded like pages were rustling. "What are these?"

"Mistakes, just like I told you," Ron said. "Simple mistakes you don't need to worry about. Trust me. It'll all be fine if you'll only trust me."

"How about if you trust me? 'Don't worry about it' isn't an answer in my book. If you want things to go back to the way they were . . ." Maura made a frustrated sound, as if she couldn't find the right words to finish her thought.

What things were to go back to how they were? Dinah's books? The Bettys? Something between Ron and Maura? Faith's brain flipped through the possible meanings of what she was hearing. Or overhearing, to be precise.

She caught the sound of footsteps coming down the stairs.

"Think about what I said," Maura told him.

"Wait. Don't go like that," Ron pleaded. "We need to talk. I—"

More footsteps. "I've said all I have to say."

Faith realized Maura was heading toward her. She ducked around the corner and out of sight.

The weight of the discussion pressed on her all the way to Dinah's suite. Was it her place to say anything? She couldn't exactly say if she'd heard a professional or a personal conversation. In fact, she shouldn't have heard the conversation in the first place. Repeating an eavesdropped exchange wasn't the kind of standard Faith held herself to.

She still hadn't decided when she knocked on the door of the Daphne du Maurier Suite.

Dinah met her at the door almost immediately, Pouf in her arms. "You just caught me. I was on my way downstairs. Oh," she said, spying the box of books Faith carried. "I had totally forgotten about those."

"Me too," Faith admitted. "I'm sorry for the delay."

"You can put them on the desk and shut the door behind you. Pouf and I have to run."

Whether or not the argument between Maura and Ron bore repeating, now certainly wasn't the time to do so. Faith slid the box onto the desk in Dinah's room.

The author and her rabbit had already disappeared down the stairs by the time Faith left the suite and closed the door.

It's not really my business anyway, is it? she wondered. *Best to let Ron and Maura sort things out for themselves.*

Her only task tonight was to go home to Watson and spend a cozy evening by the fire, digging into the first chapters of *Betty Townsend and the Morse Code Murder.*

"You'll stay home today," Faith informed Watson as she prepared to go to work the next morning. "You were a good sport yesterday, but you and I both know those rabbits could prove far too tempting. But I'll tell you what, Rumpy. I'll see if I can talk Brooke into saving a little salmon for you as a reward for your cooperation."

The promise of a salmon bribe must have done the trick, for as she grabbed her shawl and bag, Watson happily settled down on a couch cushion in spite of her use of the offensive nickname.

"I'll see you tonight," she called as she headed out her cottage door to walk across the lawn and begin the first full day of Betty Townsend Week at Castleton Manor.

Faith's short but beautiful commute was one of the best perks of this job. The manor stood regally in the morning mist, impressive even though she saw it every day. Did the Jaxons' forefather Angus have the same feeling when he spied his home at the end of nineteenth-century whaling expeditions?

Even in the pale winter light, the blue-gray roof tiles gleamed across the striking angles of the roof. Arched windows looked out onto the vast lawns and gardens—complete with requisite English hedge mazes and topiaries—while great spans of terraces waited for warm weather.

Faith found every part of the estate beautiful and inspiring, especially the picturesque gardener's cottage she was blessed to be able to call her home. She was always surrounded by elegance and a library full of amazing books. Some days she felt like she ought to pinch herself.

Let's hope this week is more like the vacation it's supposed to be and less like the civil war I fear it's turning into, she thought as she started up the great stone steps that fronted the mansion's large double-doored entrance.

"Morning, Miss Newberry," someone called out.

Faith turned to see gardener Eban Matthews standing on the terrace with a broom. The amiable young man worked part-time at the manor and often helped out with maintenance tasks during the winter months when the gardens weren't so demanding.

"You're here early," Faith replied, surprised to see Eban working first thing in the morning.

"Mack's back is acting up again, so I'm helping out. Plus," he added with a grin, "I think the rabbits sort of spook him."

"Better suited to his horse friends?" She laughed. Mack had been employed at Castleton longer than anyone else, and the elderly maintenance man was especially fond of the manor's fine horses.

"You won't hear it from me," Eban said, opening the door for her. "I think the bunnies are pretty cool. And a few of those younger fans are really cute. Think they'd knit me a scarf?"

"Have you been taking lessons in charm from Mr. Jaxon?" Faith teased. If some of the Bettys went out of their way to get to know Wolfe, it wouldn't be the first time guests had been as smitten with the estate's handsome owner as with the manor itself. If Eban learned half the social suaveness Wolfe Jaxon possessed, he'd do very well in the world indeed.

"Steer clear of Ms. Russell, by the way," Eban advised. "I think the rabbits have her spooked too."

Faith could only imagine.

The sight of the manor's entranceway always gave her a small thrill. Were Watson with her today, she would laugh at the cat's continually aloof attitude toward the building. Watson typically paid the manor no attention, as if he simply viewed the architectural wonder as appropriately worthy of his presence.

But Faith never tired of admiring the magnificent structure. Whenever she entered, she always paused to gaze at the way the huge crystal chandelier caught the light. She always marveled at the grand marble staircase that elegantly rose to a landing above. She always took a moment to appreciate the life-size statue of Agatha Christie that stood in the Great Hall Gallery.

Maybe it would have been okay to allow Watson to come along today, Faith thought as she noticed there were no rabbits in sight.

Many of the guests stood in the lobby chatting, with knitting projects or Betty Townsend novels in their hands. As before, they still seemed to divide themselves into distinct groups by age, but Faith could see little evidence of stress or hostility. This morning, they mostly ignored each other and talked in small groups like any crowd of manor guests.

She thought of Maura and the tense conversation she'd overheard yesterday. *I hope she got whatever she needed out of this morning's yoga session*, Faith mused as she waved to some of the guests and headed to the library.

Her path took her straight to Marlene. The woman stood in the middle of the lobby, arms crossed, scowling at the groups Faith had just walked past.

"They're not bringing those bunnies to breakfast, are they?" she asked, peering around Faith.

"Not that I can see," Faith replied. "You know, they seem like very nice people."

"Nice people don't eat with animals."

Faith glanced back over her shoulder. "I don't see anyone bringing their bunnies to breakfast."

"That's because I put my foot down. Did you know there was a whole group of them having afternoon tea in the salon yesterday with rabbits in their laps?"

Eban had been right about the assistant manager. This event was going to be even harder on Marlene than it would be on Watson.

"I drink tea with Watson on my lap all the time," Faith told her. "It's cozy."

"It's unsanitary," Marlene snapped. "I've no doubt we'll be vacuuming up fur and heaven knows what else for the next month." She huffed and then stared suddenly at the other end of the lobby.

Faith followed Marlene's gaze to see Watson, sitting there calmly, as if to say, "Forget someone?"

"Watson!" Faith exclaimed, then turned to Marlene. "I deliberately left him at home this morning on account of the rabbits."

"And I can see how well that turned out." Marlene glared at the cat. The assistant manager had never been fond of Watson's uncanny ability to appear and disappear at will all over the estate, and this morning was no exception. "I'd better get back to my office. We're going to need to double up on the housekeeping rounds today."

Faith wasn't sure that was true, but she had no desire to linger and argue the point with Marlene. Instead, she walked toward Watson, scolding her willful feline. "What happened to our deal? I'll let you stay, but you had better be a perfect gentleman today. No going anywhere but the library, understand?"

Watson didn't appear the least bit contrite as he followed Faith to the library.

Faith pulled her keys from her pocket, but the door swung open at her touch. "I'll have to talk with Maura about locking up after herself to keep those bunnies out."

Watson bounded ahead of her in his usual fashion.

She walked into the room and stopped at the bank of light switches. "At least she turned the lights out when she was finished."

Faith switched on the lights and turned toward the balcony.

And swallowed a scream.

There, sprawled on the floor in a tangle of limbs that had nothing to do with yoga, lay Maura Webber. She stared at the ceiling with glassy, unfocused eyes. A yoga mat was spread a few feet away. Closer to the woman lay a host of scattered books, including several of the library's largest volumes.

Faith ran toward the young woman and knelt to shake her shoulder. "Maura!" Her quick check for a pulse revealed only stillness. Even through her stylish athletic top, the editor was beginning to feel cold to the touch.

Faith wasn't a medical professional, but it didn't take one to know Maura Webber was dead.

She stood up, scanning the room for any clues as to what had happened. Aside from the littering of books around Maura's body, the library was undisturbed. Nothing from the glass cases housing the manor's rare collections seemed amiss. No windows were open, no furniture overturned, no shelves in disarray. In fact, there were no signs of struggle anywhere but around the late editor.

Faith fought for composure as the air seemed to thin out around her. A bright young woman's life had been cut woefully short. She had seemed so determined, so optimistic about the future she now would not have.

She gasped. What would this mean for the retreat, for all the work Maura had been doing? This would prove a devastating loss to her colleagues gathered here. And what about her friends and family, wherever they might be? Faith thought about the sadness that would be cast over the event and everyone involved.

"Poor Dinah," she said aloud. And Ron—was his last conversation with Maura the bitter argument she'd overheard?

What now? Obviously, she should call 911 first, but then what? Wolfe might be a better choice than poor stressed Marlene, at least for the moment. Often traveling on business, he wasn't on-site for many of the manor's events, but she was grateful he was here now.

Faith locked the library door from the inside and shut the blinds over the door's glass pane. No one should accidentally see or walk in on such a sad scene.

She dialed 911 and informed them of the situation. It seemed such a dreadful thing to pare down Maura's terrible demise to a quick relay of facts, but she knew from experience that Chief Garris or any one of the officers from the Lighthouse Bay police force would handle the situation with both efficiency and compassion.

Her fingers began to shake as she made the next call to Wolfe's private quarters on the third floor. An early riser, he'd no doubt be up and likely already working, so she wasn't surprised when he answered the phone after the first ring.

"Good morning, Faith."

"Something's very wrong."

His friendly tone changed upon hearing the alarm in hers. "What's happened?"

"I came in this morning and found Maura Webber on the library floor." She forced herself to take a deep breath before she said, "She's dead."

"She's . . . Did you just say she's dead?" Wolfe's voice was hoarse with the same shock that tightened Faith's own throat.

"I did. I found no pulse and she's cold." She glanced back at the scene. "I can't say for certain, but it looks as if she fell from the balcony."

"Have you called 911?"

"Right before I called you. I haven't checked to see if Marlene is in her office yet. How do we handle this?"

"I'll take care of Marlene. Lock the door so no guests can stray in."

"Already done."

"Good. Stay put until I get there. Don't disturb anything that might tell us what happened. I'll try and get Garris on the phone. Perhaps there's a way to handle this without sirens and anything else that might alarm the guests."

When Faith ended the call, she felt the room spin a bit. Her pulse drummed in her ears as the gravity of the situation began to sink in.

She knew it was probably less than a minute, but it felt as if an hour had gone by before Wolfe let himself in the library door.

Wolfe halted at the shocking scene before him. "What a nightmare," he whispered, breathing hard. He must have taken the back stairs at a run. "Why was she in the library so early?"

"She asked permission to use it for yoga practice," Faith said numbly. "She wanted a place where no one could find her."

"Yoga in the library?" he asked. "We have a yoga room."

"I told her that," Faith replied. "But she still wanted complete privacy and insisted on using the library."

"What an odd thing to request."

"I know, but you'd asked us to be as accommodating as possible. I went to Marlene, and she approved her use of a library key."

Wolfe ran one hand down his face, and she could practically hear his brain whir to collect the facts and decide next steps. "When did she die?"

"I don't know. I would guess it was sometime this morning. When I got here now, I found the door unlocked. I assumed she'd forgotten to lock up after herself until . . ."

For a stunned second, they were both quiet as they viewed the unfortunate scene. The elegant and peaceful atmosphere Maura had admired was long gone from the space. Instead, an eerie silence filled the richly appointed room.

Watson slipped past her legs and scurried up the stairs to the library's balcony. He meowed loudly as he peered down at them between the railings directly over Maura.

"She must have fallen over the railing," Faith said as she cast her gaze up at Watson and then followed the sharp drop to Maura's body. She nodded toward the various large books in disarray on the floor around the woman. "Those volumes are from the balcony shelves."

"I thought you said she was doing yoga, not research," Wolfe replied. "Her mat is down here. What reason would she have to be up on the balcony?"

"I have no idea." Faith put her hand to her forehead and forced herself to inhale calmly and deeply. Poor Maura. Her insistence on absolute privacy meant no one had found her in time to help her. That is, if she could have been helped at all. "It's terrible. None of this makes sense."

Wolfe pinched the bridge of his nose. "Marlene is on her way, and Garris will do his best not to alarm Dinah or our other guests."

"That won't last long," Faith said. "They'll know soon enough."

"There will have to be an investigation, interviews, that sort of thing. There's no hope of keeping it from the guests. The whole thing is bad enough, but I hate to have to announce it in the middle of a crucial event like this."

"Poor Dinah and Ron," Faith said, thinking of the distress she'd heard in the publisher's voice in the stairwell. "I don't see how this can do anything but send everyone into a state of alarm."

"We'll have to do whatever we can to try and keep things calm."

Faith thought of the Bettys and sucked in a breath as she recalled Maura's earlier words. "Maura told me she was concerned that someone would try to ruin this event. What if that person—or persons—was trying to ruin more than just the event? Maura doesn't—*didn't* strike me as the kind to overreact." It was a painful correction to make, though she hadn't even known the woman twenty-four hours.

"What are you saying?"

"Is it possible there's foul play going on here? I assumed Maura fell off the balcony, but what if she didn't fall?"

"You mean maybe someone pushed Maura off that balcony?"

"It's possible, isn't it? Maybe even more likely than a fall? She was young and in good shape. If she did yoga regularly, then she probably had decent balance as well. I don't see someone like that simply toppling over a railing for no apparent reason, do you?"

Wolfe glanced from the balcony to Maura's body. "I certainly don't like the idea, but yes, I suppose it's possible." He returned his gaze to Faith. "But who?"

"That is the question, isn't it? Maura insisted her yoga sessions were to be kept absolutely private. She told me she needed someplace she could be sure she wouldn't be interrupted. Marlene and I were the only people who knew she was here."

Faith peered up at Watson, still perched above the scene. Her cat had an extraordinary knack for finding clues to the many mysteries that had befallen the manor. She hoped he was putting that talent to use now as he gazed down, tail twitching as if in thought.

Wolfe walked carefully around the body and the scattered books. "If she was so concerned about privacy, why leave the door open? Why not lock herself in?"

"That's exactly what makes me think someone else was in here. And left in a hurry."

Wolfe pivoted to gaze out the window to the manor's front drive. "Garris should be pulling up any minute. We'll need to work with Ron and Dinah to keep the guests calm and give Garris whatever cooperation he'll need from them."

Faith walked toward her desk. "Hopefully Marlene can divert all the morning's activities away from this part of the manor."

Wolfe picked up the receiver on the phone that sat on Faith's desk. "Wait here for Garris. I'll call Ron, then go upstairs and inform him and Dinah. This will be an unpleasant business for everyone involved." He paused before dialing. "It's a shame. She seemed bright and successful for her age."

Faith slumped down at her desk while Wolfe calmly told Ron he was on his way upstairs with very serious news. She didn't envy Wolfe one bit, but she knew he would handle the situation with dignity and compassion. This proved to be yet another time she was grateful for his steady and cool composure. *Librarians are supposed to come to work and find books, not bodies.*

"Dinah will be devastated," she said as Wolfe finished his somber call. "She's lost a colleague, maybe even a good friend." She thought of Ron. Had he lost more than a colleague or friend? It was hard to say if the argument she'd overheard was a strongly worded professional argument or one of a more passionate nature. "I don't see how they can go on with the event, can you?"

Wolfe put a hand on her shoulder. "That's not our decision to make. The police will know how to handle the guests. As for the event, we'll have to take our cue from Dinah and Ron. I'd better get up there."

As he headed for the door, Faith rose and walked over to the unfortunate woman.

Watson descended from his lofty view and walked around the body and books in a slow circle the same way Wolfe had done just a few minutes ago.

"You know better than to touch anything, Rumpy," Faith warned. "But if you see something I don't . . ."

Watson stopped and sniffed at Maura's left wrist. His tail twitched rapidly, and he looked up at Faith with an expression that seemed to say, "As a matter of fact, I do."

"Wolfe," Faith called, though he was halfway out the door, "wait a minute. I think Watson's found something." She turned toward her cat. "What do you see?" Crouching down, Faith tried to follow Watson's gaze as Wolfe rejoined them.

Maura was wearing posh but otherwise unassuming exercise clothes, and she was barefoot like most people were when practicing yoga. The burgundy polish on her toes matched the shade on her manicured fingernails. Her dark hair was half-tugged out of its ponytail, and a striking necklace of a gold letter *M* hung off her neck.

But Watson wasn't looking at any of those things. He was staring at the woman's charm bracelet. It was a lovely thing, rather old and fussy-looking considering Maura's modern style. A family heirloom, perhaps?

As she peered closer, Faith's heart twisted at the *Darling Daughter* charm, as well as a tennis racket, a birthstone, and other symbols of the life now gone. "Such a loss," she said. Then she noticed something tangled around several of the charms. "Wait, look."

Watson went to paw at it, but she gently swatted him away. "Don't touch, mister."

"No contaminating evidence, even for you," Wolfe added, smiling. "What is it?"

Faith leaned in as close as she could without touching anything. "It's hairs. White hairs. Quite a few of them."

"You mean like an old woman's?" Wolfe asked.

"Yes, I suppose so," Faith replied. Her mind cast back to the collection of furry animals she'd seen yesterday. "Or a rabbit's."

5

Faith sat back and stroked Watson's fur to calm her nerves, which were still frayed from the events of the day.

Everything had moved so fast after Chief Garris arrived. While a forensics team got to work on the crime scene, the chief had announced the tragedy to the other guests and requested that all of them agree to be interviewed and not leave the manor. The guests had been shocked and horrified, and it had taken all of Wolfe's charm and Marlene's efficiency to calm them. Even then, Faith wasn't sure they would have managed if Dinah hadn't stepped in to soothe her Bettys.

Faith had just told her friends at the Candle House Book Club about the sad discovery in the manor library. They had originally planned to discuss *Betty Townsend and the Morse Code Murders* that evening during their meeting, but the day's traumatic occurrence had taken precedence.

"It's all so unfortunate." Eileen shook her head in sympathy as she worked on her knitting. "That poor young woman."

"Maura was in her thirties at the most," Faith replied. "She certainly seemed smart and very driven. She brimmed with excitement for Dinah's new direction. She told me it was going to spell great things for the both of them."

"I imagine the atmosphere at the manor is difficult right now to put it mildly," Eileen went on. "All the guests must be upset."

"Ron—he's the publisher Maura worked for—and Dinah are especially upset, of course," Faith said. "Maura was closer to them than anyone else at the event. But everyone is shaken by what's happened."

"It's rattled the staff too," Brooke added.

"My heart goes out to Dinah," Midge commiserated. "That's an awfully public spot to be in when you've just lost a colleague."

Midge's Chihuahua was a fixture at their book club meetings. This evening, Atticus was curled up in Midge's lap, and he looked rather academic, thanks to a snappy argyle sweater and his specialized pair of glasses. The Doggles helped with the little dog's vision issues.

"Maura was most likely a good friend as well as a colleague since she and Dinah worked together so much," Eileen observed.

"Dinah handled the tragedy in the most amazing way, though," Faith said. "Even upset as she was. It was sweet and sad at the same time."

"What did she do?" Eileen asked.

"No one knew what would happen with the event today," Faith answered. "I think most people felt it couldn't rightly go on. It is a death, after all. The original schedule left the afternoon open for the Bettys—that's what they call themselves—to knit and read and meet each other, and Dinah asked that they do just that."

"You mean go on with the conference?" Midge asked with something akin to horror.

Eileen frowned. "Isn't that . . . well, a bit callous given what's happened? I mean, someone died. Someone important to Dinah, her publisher, and the Bettys."

"I thought so too," Faith replied, "until Wolfe explained Dinah's viewpoint to me. Then it made sense."

"How so?" Brooke asked.

"Dinah told Wolfe that knitting and reading are what she does when she's upset. And she feels most of the Bettys would say the same. So Dinah announced they would do that today—knit and read together as a way to help each other cope with such heartbreaking news."

"I do that," Eileen agreed, holding up the beautiful blue mitten she was working on. "Knitting soothes me. I can see how therapeutic it would be to knit and read with people who are going through the same thing you are. I think it's lovely how Dinah cares about her readers."

"I have to say, it was comforting to walk around the manor this afternoon," Faith went on. "There were small groups of people talking and hugging each other, petting their rabbits, and working on their competition knitting. They were there supporting each other and Dinah."

"I suppose it's as fitting a way as any for them to honor Maura's memory," Brooke said.

"But poor Dinah," Eileen said with a sigh. "I can't imagine losing one of my employees here at the library. I'm sure her relationship with Maura was just as close, if not closer."

"Dinah did stay in her room at first, but by lunch I saw her walking among all the Bettys," Faith said. "She was giving hugs, talking, looking at competition projects, and holding lots of bunnies. She's clearly grieving, but I think it helped to be around the people she does all this for and to immerse herself in some of her favorite things."

Glancing around the room, Faith could see why Dinah had made the choice she had. After today, it really was comforting to be with friends and among books and their beloved pets. Today especially, Faith was grateful animal companions were as welcome at the book club meetings as they were at the manor.

"So Maura fell from the library balcony?" Midge asked.

"Does Chief Garris have any theories as to what happened?" Brooke said. "He spent the whole day interviewing guests and even some of the staff."

Midge's and Brooke's questions reflected the book club's other talent—solving mysteries. It was another reason Faith was so glad to be with her friends tonight after such a stressful and puzzling day.

"We don't really know what happened," Faith admitted. "If Garris has any theories, he hasn't shared them yet."

"I wonder if Maura had a medical episode of some kind," Brooke suggested. "You said she seemed intent on reducing her stress and wanted absolute privacy. Could she have been hiding a condition no one knew about?"

"It's possible," Faith answered as she got up to refill her coffee cup and select a pair of cookies for herself and a tunaroon for Watson. "I doubt we'll know anything until the police run their tests. And even that may not really tell us what happened."

Eileen glanced up from her knitting. "You don't think she was pushed, do you?"

"Now, ladies," Midge said, "not everything ends up being a murder mystery that we need to solve."

"Unfortunately, I think this might be one of them," Eileen said. "That balcony railing isn't low. It's hard to see how someone could accidentally fall over it."

"You talked to Maura," Brooke said to Faith. "Did you get the impression she had conflicts with anyone at the event?"

Faith immediately thought of the argument she'd overheard. "She had a heated discussion with Ron Powers, but nothing that sounded like it would lead to murder."

Eileen made a derisive sound. "I'll bet some of the guests had issues with Maura. I've read the reviews online. Lots of Betty fans are upset with the way this new editor is shifting Dinah's career."

"Sounds like you might be too," Midge commented.

Eileen paused in her handiwork. "If we're going to go ahead and discuss the book, then I'll start by telling you I didn't like it nearly as much as Dinah's other ones."

"Really?" Brooke asked. "I thought it was great. A dashing hero, a heartwarming romance in the glamour of historic New York City—what's not to like?"

"That's because you love that romantic stuff," Eileen replied, "and you haven't read the other Betty Townsend novels. This one was okay, but the ones before it are so much better. After so many books, readers have expectations for an author, and I felt that this book didn't measure up."

"I liked it," Midge offered. "Before I read it, I didn't know anything about telephone operators from that era. It seems so much more interesting to be connected by a real person than to hit an icon on my smartphone."

"I cried when Betty said goodbye to the orphans to head for New York," Eileen admitted. "I just don't see how a Betty Townsend novel can be a Betty Townsend novel without the orphanage. What did you think, Faith?"

"I got halfway through it last night, and I had planned to finish it this afternoon. As you can imagine, I didn't get the chance. Does Betty decide to stay in New York to be with Lieutenant Drake?"

Eileen stared at Faith. "You want us to tell you the end?" Her expression made it clear that this was a cardinal sin of reading.

"Normally I wouldn't ask, but I'm not very likely to get the chance to finish it now. And it'd be better if I could talk about it intelligently in front of Dinah if it comes up."

"Betty abandons the orphanage for a new career in New York City at a big office building with Lieutenant Drake." From Eileen's tone, it was obvious that she did not consider it a satisfying plot development.

"Don't put it that way," Brooke protested, then turned to Faith. "Betty embarks on an exciting new career with the man she loves in the dazzling society of New York City. It's a great read. You should get back to it when you have the time."

"I doubt it will happen anytime soon," Faith replied. "Not with a death at the manor."

Midge let Atticus off her lap to settle snugly at her feet. "Not just a death, but a mysterious death. You've got a mystery writer with a real-life mystery on her hands."

"Mysterious or not," Eileen said, "it's still a terrible thing to have happened. I feel for Dinah. The event can't help but be ruined, and I've got to think the Bettys look forward to this all year. I know I was excited about the charity book signing."

Faith had secured a ticket to the event so Eileen could meet her favorite author. "I believe the charity book signing and the rest of Betty Townsend Week will continue as planned."

"Even after what's happened?" Eileen sounded surprised. "You explained why they went ahead with their activities this afternoon, but I assumed they'd cancel the rest of them."

"Marlene says that while things may change, as of today they're not canceling," Brooke said. "She told me to keep with the schedule for tomorrow's events and the rest of the week until I hear otherwise."

"I was wondering what would happen to all those batches of my new rabbit-friendly carrot cookies," Midge said. "I'm glad to know they won't go to waste. In fact, I might even have to whip up some more."

Faith had always admired how creative her friend could get with her pet bakery. Not only were tunaroons the fastest way to Watson's heart, but Midge was always dreaming up new ways for all sorts of pet owners to treat the animals they loved. Her knowledge as a vet meant the treats were always safe for animals.

"Really?" Eileen asked.

Midge nodded. "Dinah Harper called me this afternoon and ordered cookie gift packs to be delivered to each of the manor guest rabbits every day for the rest of the week."

"Along with the extra snacks and pampering she's requested for the human guests," Brooke said. "Dinah sounds like an amazing woman, going out of her way to make everyone feel better despite what has to be a personal tragedy."

"Evidently the rabbits get to stress eat alongside their humans," Midge remarked. "I'm glad for the sales but not under such sad circumstances."

"What else do they have planned for the week?" Eileen asked.

"Various programs, rabbit shows, knitting competitions—"

"Wait," Midge interrupted. "Knitting is a competitive sport?"

"It is to the Bettys," Eileen replied. "Bettys take their knitting and their choice of yarn very seriously."

Faith was glad she could manage a small laugh. "It's the most unique part of the whole event if you ask me. Evidently, angora yarn comes from Angora bunnies, like Dinah's in real life and Betty's in the books.

Most of the fans own rabbits, and they brought them to the retreat."

"You should see them," Brooke said. "All sizes and colors. Some of them have so much fur it's hard to see the rabbit underneath. Seriously, there were a few with hair twice as long as mine."

Faith thought of Beatrice and her championship coat. Francine had let her hold the animal that afternoon, and it was splendidly soft. It would calm anyone to spend a few minutes stroking the dear rabbit.

Don't you worry, Watson, she thought as she stroked the beloved cat who had seen her through thick and thin over the years. *I don't have any plans to trade you in for a fuzzy bunny.*

Watson purred in response.

"One of the Bettys explained the whole event to me this afternoon," Faith said. "The week includes lots of book-related workshops and such, but it also has a rabbit show and an angora yarn knitting competition."

"What kind of competition?" Midge asked.

"The contestants can make whatever they want," Faith answered. "But it must be from angora or angora-blend yarn—some from their own rabbits, even—and it must be knit entirely at the event. I saw one woman starting a project as she walked in the door, before she even made it up to her room."

"I read that last year's winner knit an entire baby layette during the week of the event. Onesie, beanie, booties, and even a blanket," Eileen said. "I can't imagine doing something like that in only a week."

Faith settled back in her chair. "It sounds like it's going to be a busy week for all of us."

"It is," Brooke agreed. "I think even Marlene is stressed. She needs an hour with a cuddly bunny to calm her nerves. Not that she'd ever do such a thing."

"The rabbits are a large part of why she's stressed," Faith said.

Midge laughed. "I can just imagine Marlene's reaction to all those rabbits everywhere. I think she has enough trouble embracing cats and dogs as guests."

"She even gave Diva and Bling the evil eye," Brooke said. Diva and Bling were her pet angelfish. "She came over to my house to deliver some paperwork once when I was sick, and they wouldn't eat when she was there. In fact, they binge ate after she'd left."

"Maura's death did put Marlene over the edge, I'm afraid," Faith said. "She told Chief Garris she expected him to make a statement ruling out any sort of foul play by dinner tonight."

"Did he?" Midge asked.

Faith shook her head. "I don't think they can come to that conclusion so fast, but Marlene was snarling at Garris anyway. I'm always glad to be with you all, but I was especially grateful to have a reason to be off the grounds tonight."

"Then it really *is* a mystery if they can't rule out foul play," Eileen declared.

"They can't rule out anything yet," Faith said. "Garris told Wolfe there are some tests they run about how Maura fell that can suggest if it was an accident or if she was pushed. Still, those tests take time. He's going to go through with them, but I don't think he's convinced that there's a reason to be suspicious."

"Aren't there always reasons to be suspicious?" Eileen said.

"You really need to read more romance novels," Brooke told her. "You need a bigger dose of happily ever after."

Eileen had, in fact, had a wonderful marriage before becoming a widow. She was one of the kindest, most vibrant people Faith knew.

"I, for one, appreciate Eileen's nose for mystery as much as I appreciate Watson's," Faith said, coming to her aunt's defense. "But there weren't any signs of a struggle that I could see."

"You told me you found several huge books around her," Eileen persisted.

There were days Faith had to wonder if the book club let their sleuthing imaginations run away with them. But she also trusted their instincts, and the group had played a large part in solving more than one mystery in Lighthouse Bay. Above all that, Faith's gut was telling her it was entirely possible Maura Webber didn't fall by accident.

Still, this was a time to be cautious about jumping to conclusions without enough information. A death during an event was bad enough. A murder would be even worse.

"True," Faith replied. "But she could have been holding the books when she fell. She was a small woman, so their weight might have been enough to topple her off-balance and over the balcony."

"That sounds rather unlikely," Midge said. "What were the books about?"

Faith shrugged. "A variety of unrelated subjects. I think Maura would have asked me for help if she'd been doing research."

"So there was nothing in common about the books?" Midge asked.

"Well, there was one thing they all had in common," Faith replied.

"What was that?" Eileen said eagerly.

"All of them were large and heavy."

"Good weapons," Brooke added.

"Murder weapons," Eileen announced.

"That's not a real clue," Midge declared, crossing her arms. "Most books up in that balcony are large and heavy." She turned to Faith. "Was there anything truly suspicious?"

"I don't know about suspicious," Faith said, "but I was hoping you could help with a particular clue."

"You know I'll do anything to help," Midge replied.

Faith pulled out her cell phone and brought up a picture she had snapped that morning, then handed it to Midge. "Watson pointed out to me that Maura was wearing a charm bracelet when she died."

"Who wears fancy jewelry doing predawn yoga?" Brooke asked.

"I thought it was odd too," Faith replied. "Maura was wearing exercise clothes and didn't have any makeup on. I'd guess it must be something precious to her that she never took off."

"So how is this a clue?" Midge asked.

Faith enlarged the image of the bracelet. "See those hairs tangled up in it?"

Midge squinted at the photo. "Oh, now I do. The long white ones."

"As a vet, would you be able to tell if the hairs belonged to a rabbit?"

"Do you know they're not human?" Eileen asked. "What if they belong to Maura's killer?"

"Garris did take them as evidence, but that still doesn't mean Maura was killed," Faith answered.

"If Garris would let me study one of the hairs under a microscope," Midge said, "I could tell you what animal they came from." She glanced up from the phone. "Most species have distinct characteristics in their hair and fur."

"But could you tell between breeds of Angora rabbits?"

Midge cocked her head. "Now that's getting a bit tricky. I'd have to do some research, but I think there are a handful of Angora breeds. It's not like I have a DNA lab behind the bakery." She gave Faith a dubious look. "Surely you're not suggesting Maura was attacked by bunnies?"

"Of course not. But that bracelet and the hairs on it—whomever they belong to, human or rabbit—are the only clue we've got so far."

6

Faith had seen many unusual things in her tenure as the librarian at Castleton Manor, but the collection of rabbits, Bettys, and yarn that filled the manor's rooms Wednesday as part of Betty Townsend Week topped the list.

Bunnies covered the lawn. Bettys knitted in the music room and the salon. Guests paraded their rabbits around the lobby and the gallery. Wolfe told Faith that he'd even found one guest hopping her rabbit on a treadmill in the gym.

Someone had knitted a small red heart with Maura's initials and placed it as a makeshift memorial in one hand of the Agatha Christie statue. That "decoration" had taxed Marlene's tolerance. Hours later when some daring soul "yarn-bombed" the statue by draping a bright blue angora scarf around Agatha's neck, Marlene nearly hyperventilated.

Usually, events such as this brought many guests to the library during their stay. In this instance, Faith found herself more at peace than usual, if one didn't count the lingering memory of a departed editor sprawled across the library floor.

Dinah and Ron had opted to cancel only the seminars and discussions involving Maura, so attendees still had a wide variety of literary and fiber activities to choose from.

Garris had warned most of the guests away from gaping at the scene of the accident, but a few still wandered into the library to view the collection of Dinah's books as well as the selection of the books related to yarn and rabbits that Faith had put out on special display. She was grateful that only a daring few inquired about Maura's accident—it wasn't anything she cared to recount often. For the most part, the manor guests seemed to be coping with the tragedy by focusing on their needlework, their pets, and each other instead of finding solace in the library.

Wolfe stopped by the library just before lunch. "Everything back in order?" he asked with a glance at the clearing below the balcony that had been such a disturbing scene yesterday.

"More or less, since it's been so quiet in here today," Faith replied. "The bindings on the two biggest books were ripped beyond my skills to fix when they fell, so I'm sending them out for repairs. The rest of the minor dings I could handle, so everything else has been put to rights. Except, of course, for how Maura died."

Wolfe sat down opposite Faith's desk, telling her this was more than a social call. "Well, that's one of the reasons I came to see you. For one, I wanted to make sure you'd recovered okay. It's quite a shock to find a body in your library. I know this place is your sanctuary."

Wolfe's caring nature was one of the things Faith liked most about the man. He cared a great deal about everyone who worked for him, and he went out of his way to show it. Faith often thought the world would be a much nicer place with more men like him in it.

"Thanks for your concern, but while I can't say these have been the calmest days I've had, I'm fine."

"I'm glad to hear it," Wolfe said. "I'm also astounded that the guests seem as calm as they are. You'll need to tell Midge her delivery of those rabbit cookie packs went a long way in improving guest morale. Or is it rabbit morale? Regardless, I'm glad there's no panic. There really must be something to the rabbits and the yarn thing. Maybe I should give it a whirl."

Faith laughed. "Somehow I can't picture you knitting. Or with a bunny on your lap."

He laughed as well. "Then maybe I shouldn't. But if I had to choose between upset guests and guests with long ears and yarn in tow, I'll take the latter. Marlene's rattled enough for all of them put together."

"I think Agatha's new scarf was the last straw for her. Or would that be the last needle?" she joked. It felt good to laugh with a friend after all the tension of yesterday.

"I heard her asking Mack to have the electrical cords in the parlor wrapped in tinfoil."

"Why?"

"To keep them from being nibbled on by rabbits," Wolfe replied.

"Is that really necessary?"

He winced. "This is Marlene we're talking about. The woman gives new meaning to the word *thorough*."

"Don't you think the guests will be offended that we're taking defensive measures against their pets?"

"I asked her the same thing. She said she got the idea from one of the guests when this woman's rabbit began investigating a lamp cord in the music room."

Faith pictured Marlene stalking the parlors, watching for misbehaving rabbits, pouncing on any to protect the manor from what she viewed as its certain rodent demise.

"I'm sure that sent Marlene running for the tinfoil," Faith said. "But I've seen nothing but excellent behavior on the part of the rabbits and their owners. I even had one Betty offer to knit me an angora scarf. After the competition is over, of course."

Wolfe smiled, but his eyes remained troubled.

"What else is on your mind?" she asked.

He grinned, and this time it reached his eyes. "You always could read me like a book."

"I am a librarian, after all."

Wolfe's face turned serious again. "I had a call from Chief Garris. It seems between the autopsy and an examination of the scene, he believes that Maura was pushed."

Faith felt a chill skitter across her skin. An accident was unfortunate enough as it was, but to know the poor woman had been murdered darkened everything. "How could he know?"

"He went into a lot of technicalities I doubt I could relate accurately, but mostly it seemed that there were signs of struggle on her arms and throat, the location of the fall, and something about the angle and the force of the impact being greater than a fall ought to produce."

Someone had murdered Maura Webber. She hadn't fallen or slipped or had any kind of medical episode. She'd been deliberately pushed off the balcony to her death. By someone who could still be at the manor.

"Have you told Dinah or Ron?" she asked.

She'd shared with both Wolfe and Chief Garris about the strong words she'd heard between Ron and Maura, and it was disconcerting to think Ron might have taken things as far as violence. Or anyone—for in truth, they had no idea who the murderer was.

If the white hairs in the bracelet were indeed a clue, Ron had dark hair and didn't own a rabbit, much less a white one. Or maybe Maura had held one of the four-legged guests and hadn't noticed the white hairs. Every detail seemed more drastic and less clear in light of the disturbing news.

"Garris is coming up to let them know. He may want to look in here again, since they now have an approximate time of death—somewhere between five and five thirty that morning. It's upsetting enough that the guests know there's been a death. I worry we won't be able to keep the current level of calm once they learn it was murder."

"A murder one of them committed," Faith said. "It would almost have to be one of the overnight guests. I doubt any of the day guests would be able to come onto the estate unnoticed at that hour. It had to be someone who was already on the grounds."

Ron's suspicious argument was far from proof he was the murderer, especially in light of the white hairs, and suddenly the convivial gatherings of knitting and reading going on all over the estate didn't seem quite so cozy. No one had left, so it was entirely possible that one of those sweet, devoted, rabbit-toting Bettys was a killer.

Faith shivered. "It's a bit creepy to think about it."

"Garris will need to conduct more interviews now that this is a murder investigation," Wolfe said.

Faith gazed out the windows at the expanse of the estate. Lighthouse Bay had been graced with another unusually warm day, and even now she could see some Bettys gathered around rabbits in their pens. "A murder at a murder mystery convention. There aren't enough fuzzy bunnies in the world to make this okay."

There were times when she was grateful her cottage residence was one of the manor's outbuildings. Usually she was glad to get away from the busy conferences, but today she was thankful not to be living under the same roof as a murderer. Of course, that meant Wolfe was doing exactly that, which was reason enough to make her pulse jump.

"Did the chief mention finding Maura's cell phone?" Faith asked. "I didn't see it in here."

"When they searched her room, they didn't locate the phone," Wolfe said. "Although a GPS ping told them it was somewhere on the grounds."

"That's strange," Faith said. "I wonder where it could be."

"No idea."

They were silent for a moment.

"I suppose it's a good thing Garris has told the guests not to leave," Faith murmured. "As frightening as it is to be shut up in a building with a killer, it'll hopefully make it easier for them to catch whoever did it, once they figure out who that is."

Wolfe nodded. "It's another reason why Dinah has chosen to keep as close to the original event schedule as possible. It's better for everyone if the guests are occupied."

Faith remembered the clue Watson had found. "Did Chief Garris mention whether they'd found out anything about the hair on Maura's bracelet?"

"He did," Wolfe replied. "But I'm not sure it's any help. He told me they're waiting on confirmation, but he's almost certain it's not human hair, so they're working on the theory that it's rabbit hair."

Faith reached into her desk for her cell phone. "I'll call Midge and tell her to go ahead and ask for one of the hairs from the police station evidence files. She says she might be able to confirm if it's rabbit hair and maybe even which breed of Angora. And there's always the color. That's got to narrow it down some."

"Meaning only rabbits with long white hair." Wolfe stood up, checking his watch. "That's quite a few of our bunny guests, by my estimation. There have to be a dozen long-haired white rabbits out there."

"Right now, it's the only clue we've got. We might as well start there. Since many of the Bettys are wearing event name tags, I should be able to make a quick list of the guests whose rabbits have long white hair. Who knows? Maybe I'll decide to need impromptu knitting lessons so I can mingle. It's not much, but it's something."

"I'm going to meet with Garris up in my office. I'll come find you afterward and tell you what I've learned." He stopped at the door. "I don't need to tell you to be careful. Solving murders is Chief Garris's job, not yours, and no one wants to see you put in any danger."

"The real danger is not knowing who pushed Maura off that balcony," Faith replied. "The faster we can find our killer, the better off everyone will be."

For the next two hours, Faith mingled among the Bettys, taking discreet notice of each guest's pet rabbit.

Pearl Quinton, the club vice president who had given her such a chilly reception on her first day, hadn't warmed much. "Dreadful news about Maura's accident," Pearl said, needles flying through some elaborate-looking knitting while Lady Latte sat on her lap.

"It is sad, isn't it?" Faith sat down, impressed by the woman's speedy fingers.

"Certainly, no one likes to hear of such a thing," the older woman said as she stitched. "But what I found just as sad about this year's event is that Claudia isn't here."

Faith could hardly equate the two facts. "Claudia Ferguson? Dinah's former editor?" she asked.

"So you know about her. She was Dinah's faithful editor for every one of the Betty Townsend novels."

"Until now, of course," another Betty chimed in bitterly.

Pearl sighed. "Claudia is a delightful woman."

"And an accomplished knitter," the woman across from Pearl said. She sat stroking a gray rabbit with velvety black ears and face.

"She always attended these events, you know. A woman I considered a friend. It's not the same since she *retired*." Pearl gave the last word a very dubious emphasis. Clearly, it was widely known that Claudia's exit hadn't been entirely voluntary.

"Was Claudia invited?" Faith inquired, smiling as Lady Latte twitched a pink nose at her extended hand.

"Dinah is a gracious woman. I'm sure she wanted to invite Claudia. Maybe even tried to. But I'm equally sure that Maura put the kibosh on that. Besides, given the circumstances, would you come?"

"If Claudia felt forced out of her job, then no," she admitted. "I'm not sure that I would come. Perhaps after a year or two, when the sting died down."

Another Betty harrumphed and put down her knitting. "Pearl, stop that." Her rabbit was white with gray ears. The assortment of colors really was amazing. "Remember what Francine said."

That caught Faith's attention. "What did Francine say?"

The woman returned to her knitting as she spoke. "Francine asked us to give Maura our support. To remember that Dinah's success is a success for all Betty fans." She completed a row and gave them all a conspiratorial smile as she turned her work. "Why, I heard Francine say there was going to be a big announcement at this year's event. I'm wondering if it's a movie deal. Wouldn't that be fabulous?"

Excited murmurs filled the small circle of women.

Faith tried to ask the next question as casually as possible. "All your rabbits are so beautiful. But it does seem as if white is the most common color. Is that true? Or is it just a favorite of the Bettys?"

"Betty Townsend's rabbit is white," Pearl said with authority. "So yes, I suppose there are lots of white ones here for that reason. And the white fur is the easiest to dye, if you like those wild colors the young people favor these days." Once again, she inclined her head in the direction of a younger group of knitters across the room working with vibrantly colored yarns. "But mostly, you choose your bunny for what you like. I love coffee, so it wasn't hard to pick Lady out of the litter."

So white rabbits were among the most commonly owned. It certainly seemed that way as she'd walked through the manor that morning. Color might not help narrow down whose rabbit's fur was tangled in Maura's bracelet after all.

But length could. The hairs in that bracelet were long—much longer than the fur of any rabbit among Pearl's companions. Faith motioned to a rabbit across the room with an impressive long coat of smoky-gray fur. "Could they all get fur that long?"

"A coat like that demands lots of upkeep," Pearl said. "I mean, Angora rabbits require a lot of upkeep anyway, since they need regular grooming, shearing, and even special diets."

"They sound like a great deal of work," Faith said.

Pearl nodded. "Most Angora breeds require daily brushing and weekly blowouts to make sure they don't have loose hair building up. Rabbits groom themselves, but when their hair is this long, they can't digest it, and it can build up in their stomachs and become fatal. That's called wool block, and you have to do whatever you can to avoid it."

"How awful," Faith whispered.

"That's why you can't go into ownership of an Angora without doing your homework," Pearl said sternly, as if Faith had been considering that very thing. "And they have to be sheared every three months, or they get stressed and overheated, and the risk of wool block increases. I'll need to shear Lady Latte when we get home. The other fans and I usually time our shearings for right after this convention."

"What about the special diet?" Faith wanted to know.

"They need a lot of protein because of their wool production," Pearl answered, "and they demand a lot of fiber to help them pass any loose hairs they might ingest. They also need access to fresh hay and water."

"I had no idea something so small could be such a big job," Faith said, studying Lady Latte with new respect.

"That doesn't even touch on the shearing or plucking—depending on the breed—or spinning the wool into yarn, dyeing it if you choose to do that, and selling or using it yourself. They're almost a full-time job by themselves. But they're worth it. After all," Pearl added, smiling down at Lady Latte with the first warm expression Faith had seen on her face, "a bunny is mostly to love."

"The wonderful yarn is just a bonus," a third Betty said, holding up a pair of socks in progress.

I'd never stress another day with those fuzzy things on my feet, Faith thought. *Until Watson attacked my toes every waking moment, that is.*

"How many championship coats do you think are here this year?" Faith asked.

"Are you looking to own a rabbit?" the sock knitter asked enthusiastically.

"I don't think my cat would approve."

Faith's reply earned horrified looks from the group. Clearly, cats were not a favorite pet among this crowd.

"I should think not," Pearl said with a scowl.

"I'm mostly curious," Faith went on. "I find the whole thing fascinating."

"Well, not counting Beatrice and Lady Latte, I'd say there are a dozen other quality contenders this year." Pearl narrowed her eyes in thought. "Eight whites, a lovely gray, a pair of splendid browns, and an outrageous multi."

"That's Pearl for you," the owner of the gray rabbit said. "She can always pick the finalists."

"But you think Beatrice will defend her title?" Faith asked.

"Of course I do. She is quite honestly the finest specimen here. Always has been. No one can hold a candle to Beatrice."

"Except maybe Lady Latte," the sock knitter generously said.

The other women agreed. "Most of us would be thrilled to place in the top five. No one really thinks they'll win as long as Francine's in the contest."

"In any case," Faith said as she stood up, "Beatrice is an impressive rabbit, I agree. Thanks for teaching me so much, ladies."

"Anytime," Pearl said. "And anytime you'd like to take up knitting, you know where to find us."

Everywhere, Faith thought as she scanned the first floor of the manor. Rabbits and yarn were everywhere. But according to Pearl, there were only eight rabbits with championship white fur long enough to have been tangled in Maura's bracelet. It wasn't conclusive as far as clues went, but it gave her something to go on.

Resisting the urge to wander the grounds and catalog those eight other rabbits and their owners, Faith opted to head upstairs instead and share her findings with Wolfe.

She ran straight into him escorting a teary-eyed Dinah from his private office with Chief Garris in tow.

"I'm so very sorry about all that's happened, Dinah," Wolfe said. "Please let us know if there's anything we can do."

"We'll do everything we can to wrap this case up as quickly as possible," the chief promised. "I'll be informing the guests right now. I know it's difficult, but I agree it's best that you keep things going as much as you can."

Dinah straightened her shoulders. "The Bettys are strong. They'll pull together for each other. But I'll tell you this—I simply won't believe one of them could be the culprit." She pointed at the chief. "Find out who did this and bring them to justice."

Faith usually saved her visits to the manor's coffee bar and gift shop for the mornings, but today she decided an afternoon jolt of caffeine was necessary.

After a quick check on things in the library, she walked to the little shop tucked away on the ocean side of the manor. She thought of Lady Latte as she ordered a large mocha latte. Today was definitely a day for chocolate. And when the manager, Iris Alden, suggested adding a pair of decadent chocolate chip cookies, Faith readily agreed.

Heading out of the shop with her bolstering beverage and treats, Faith ran into Brooke coming from the tea service that had been set up each afternoon in the salon. Compared to most of the massive rooms in the manor, the salon was cozy with wood floors and pale walls. It was a favorite spot for manor guests.

"Wow," Brooke said, adjusting the strings on her apron. "These Bettys sure have a sweet tooth. I've had to double the amount of baked goods we agreed to set out. Iris is lucky she has anything left to sell."

Faith laughed. "There weren't any blueberry muffins left just now, but I was in the mood for chocolate anyway. How's the atmosphere in there?" She gestured toward the salon. "Tense?"

"Not as much as you'd think," Brooke replied.

"Well, they do love mystery novels, after all."

"And it seems they love mysteries in real life too. I wouldn't be surprised if we have a dozen amateur sleuths in the crowd snooping around for clues."

Faith pulled Brooke into the nearby butler's pantry and shut the door behind them. "After what I've heard today, they should be snooping," she whispered despite the closed space. "Wolfe told me earlier that they've established Maura was pushed off the balcony."

"So it *is* murder," Brooke said with wide eyes.

Faith nodded. "And that means the killer is most likely still here, because as far as we know, no one's left."

Brooke stared at her. "A murder among a group of divided, unhappy mystery novel fans. This is going to get interesting fast."

"I know. I was hoping it'd get *less* interesting and *less* threatening. Today I had two women ask to see the place where Maura's body landed and the balcony we know she fell from. That's not the kind of library tour I like to give."

"Wait," Brooke said. "It's a crime scene now, isn't it? Should it be roped off with yellow tape and all?"

Faith broke off a piece of cookie and popped it into her mouth. "Chief Garris is done there. They've gotten everything they can from the scene. Wolfe and I thought it best to take our cue from Dinah and keep everything open and back to normal as soon as we could."

"Is there anything for them to see anyway?"

"Not really. The only lasting evidence is the damage I've had to repair on some of those volumes. The one clue we have—which isn't much of a clue at all—is the bracelet and the fur on it."

Brooke sighed. "Never a dull moment here, is there?" She checked her watch and reached for the pantry door. "I've got to get more desserts ready for dinner tonight. Keep me posted on everything." She stopped with the door halfway open. "So they're sure it's fur and not human hairs?"

Faith followed her out into the hallway. "Almost certain, and

Midge will do what she can to help confirm that. Wolfe told me they're operating under the assumption that those hairs are rabbit fur."

A Betty, talking in loving tones to the large brown rabbit she was holding, came out of the gift shop and crossed the hallway in front of them.

"Well, there's plenty of rabbits to go around these days," Brooke said in a low voice, watching the guest. "I'm starting to think—"

A scream came from the center of the building.

Faith and Brooke looked at each other, then dashed toward the main hall.

Two more screams followed, coming from the main stairway. They were joined by several people yelling.

Faith and Brooke reached the main lobby to see Francine rushing down the stairs with something bundled in a bath towel.

"There's been an attack!" Francine shouted.

7

Faith and Brooke dashed toward the commotion, reaching the bottom of the stairs just as another woman came to the top of the landing, carrying a similar bundle. "Brutal!" she cried. "Heartless and brutal! My sweet Powder!"

As the crowd of Bettys gathered around Francine and the other woman, Faith noticed that while both bundles had long ears, their faces no longer had the fluffy elegance she'd noticed on Beatrice and the other rabbits.

"They've been sheared!" a third woman shouted as she appeared at the top of the stairs. She swayed a little as if she might topple over. "Who would do such a horrible thing to Count Cotton?"

"What do you mean?" Faith asked as she made her way over to Francine, though she was afraid she already knew.

"This," Francine said gravely and lifted the towel to show her precious Beatrice.

The animal was shivering, both from fear and likely from the fact that its magnificent fur had been haphazardly clipped, as if someone had quickly and ruthlessly taken a pair of scissors to the animal's championship coat.

"Oh, the poor thing!" Faith didn't notice any signs of actual injury to the animal, so the harm was hopefully only cosmetic. But it was clear that all three owners considered it an act of brutality.

Cries of shock and horror filled the entryway as a crowd of Bettys gathered around the victims.

Francine covered Beatrice again, shielding her as if the animal were naked, and protectively clutched the bundle to her chest.

The crowd parted as Dinah arrived. "Mercy, Francine. What's been done to Beatrice?"

71

"Her coat, her championship coat, has been stolen!" Francine wailed.

"And ours!" the two other victims cried.

Dinah reached out to grasp Francine's shaking shoulder. "How awful! Is she all right? Has she been harmed?"

"I don't think so, but her coat is destroyed," Francine moaned. "She's been traumatized. Attacked. Who would do such a terrible thing?"

"Whoever killed Maura, that's who!" someone yelled.

"We're all in danger!" someone else shouted.

Faith exchanged glances with Brooke. The question of how long it would take for the Bettys to succumb to panic had just been answered. Dinah and Ron—and perhaps the entire manor staff—had a crisis on their hands whether they liked it or not.

Dinah straightened her shoulders and turned to face the group of alarmed fans. "I know this is all very upsetting. It's a terrible thing that Maura was taken from us. And I assure you, the police are already hard at work on the case. But we are not in danger."

"How can you say that? The investigation hasn't stopped this, has it?" Pearl jabbed a finger at the trio of wrapped rabbits.

Dinah held up her hands to the group. "Yes, this is disturbing, and I know we're all frightened. But let's try not to let our emotions get the better of us. We need to do our best to be brave and calm."

"Why don't I call our concierge veterinarian so she can come and make sure the rabbits have come to no harm?" Faith asked.

"No harm?" the second rabbit owner said. "They've absolutely been harmed."

"No physical harm," Faith clarified. "Other than the robbery of their fur," she said, using Francine's term.

"Which is harm enough. It's unthinkable." The woman gestured to the two other victims. "These were all championship contenders. How could one Betty do this to another just to get a trophy?"

"It's disgraceful," Francine said. "It's beneath a Betty."

"This has never happened before," Pearl said with a sneer. "Obviously, this group isn't what it used to be." She stared straight at a group of younger fans when she spat out those last words.

Annette Higgins stepped out defiantly from the younger group. "No Betty would ever do this to a rabbit or a fellow Betty," she said firmly.

"Who else could it be?" Pearl flung her hand in a wide gesture around the group.

"We don't know," Dinah said, her voice calm. "So let's not jump to any conclusions, shall we?" She turned to the three rabbit owners. "Come upstairs to my suite. We'll wait there for the veterinarian."

"I want to file a police report," one of the owners said. "This is an act of animal vandalism. A robbery. Angora fur is worth a pretty penny."

Faith made a mental note to contact Wolfe, Marlene, Midge, and Chief Garris in that order if not simultaneously.

Brooke must have read her thoughts because she spoke up. "I'll call Midge and Chief Garris. Faith will talk to Wolfe and Marlene." She put a hand out to Dinah. "I'll have tea and extra towels sent up to your suite right away, Ms. Harper."

"We'll do everything we can to ensure your rabbits and their owners get whatever they need," Faith reassured.

But in truth, how could this be set right? The rabbits' championship coats were gone. Damaged beyond repair, at least before the competition. The poor animals resembled sheared sheep, their pink limbs and torsos shockingly small compared to when they'd had a full coat of fur. She'd have been just as upset had someone taken an electric razor to Watson, and as far as she knew, his fur didn't have any monetary value. Francine was right. It was a terribly cruel thing to do.

As Dinah led the trio of owners up to her suite, Faith headed for Marlene's office, texting Wolfe to meet her there right away.

"Sheared?" Marlene gaped at Faith as they walked to the entrance to meet Chief Garris a short while later. "As in cut all their fur off?"

"Their championship fur, to be exact," Wolfe added. "It can hardly be an accident that three of the top contenders were singled out."

"Who knew the competition would get so fierce?" Faith said.

"You never liked Peggy," one Betty snapped to another in the music room as they passed. "You always said no one ever took third place but her."

"I never said that," came a shrill reply.

"I heard you say it yesterday. You know, when Peggy's rabbit still had his hair."

Faith peered into the music room to see a group of Bettys facing off. It was the third argument she'd heard since the shearing happened. The Bettys had managed to hold their calm when a murder was committed, but it was clear today's development had pushed the group's strain over the edge.

"They're everywhere," Marlene moaned quietly as they passed yet another group of guests holding their rabbits close. The creatures were even more evident than before, as no Betty wanted to leave her precious bunny out of her sight for fear of further shearings. "Orders for room service have tripled, since we absolutely cannot allow animals in the dining room."

Wolfe pushed out a frustrated breath. "We need to find a way to get things under control and fast. Dinah's willing to do anything that might help. She's pulled in several of the fan leaders to help keep the peace, but none of that will do as much good as figuring out who is behind all this."

"I couldn't agree more," Faith said as they reached the entrance door where Chief Garris's cruiser and Midge's SUV had pulled up.

"I think I made it into my office all of five minutes before you called me back," Garris said as Wolfe let the chief and the veterinarian in through the doors. "You're taking up my entire week."

"Not by choice," Wolfe said with a grimace.

"And now you want me to investigate the theft of . . . rabbit fur?" Garris asked, raising an eyebrow.

"I don't think it's necessary," Marlene said. "The whole event is just plain ridiculous."

Faith was glad the woman kept her voice low given the high-running emotions in the building.

"You don't think any of the rabbits have been hurt?" Midge asked. The veterinarian's bright-red fingernails, with a paw print on each thumb, flashed as she readjusted her grip on her black medical bag.

"We don't know," Faith answered, glad to see the compassion that filled Midge's eyes. Unusual or not, the whole business did seem mean-spirited and extreme. But if anyone would know what to do for the animals and say to fearful owners, Midge would. "They don't appear to be harmed. Other than shaken up and—well, cold. The owners are certainly upset."

"As they should be." Midge scowled. "Who'd do something like that?"

Garris scanned the lobby. "Any shears or the like reported missing from the pet spa?"

"I hadn't thought to look," Wolfe replied. "Let's go talk to the staff and see if any equipment has disappeared."

The two of them headed off in the direction of the pet spa.

"Where are the victims and their owners now?" Midge asked.

Faith gestured to the staircase. "Upstairs. Dinah's gathered them in the Daphne du Maurier Suite, where she's staying."

"I had hoped to meet Dinah Harper under happier circumstances," Midge remarked as she ascended the stairs. "I've discovered I really do like her books. I've started another one since our book club meeting, and I'll probably read the whole series."

Faith grinned at her friend. "Am I looking at a future Betty?"

"Fan, yes. Going so far as to do the bunny thing, I don't think so. Unless it's a breed that's easy to care for." She glanced around the collection of guests and rabbits milling around the lobby. "Mercy, some of these are twice the size of Atticus."

The vet's beloved Chihuahua was a feisty little guy with loads of character, and Midge loved him to distraction, but Faith thought that saying an animal was bigger than Atticus wasn't exactly impressive. Snickerdoodles Bakery & Tea Shop, a favorite gathering spot of the book club, sold larger loaves of bread.

"They're not so big when you get the fur off," Faith replied, remembering the image of poor Beatrice devoid of her championship coat. "They're as tiny as Atticus underneath, poor creatures."

Midge gave Faith a dubious glance.

"No, really," Faith insisted. "It's a shocking change. Beatrice looks nothing like her elegant self without all that fluff. I'd be distraught if someone did that to Watson."

"Downright undignified, bless their little furry hearts," Midge said. "Let's go make sure everyone's okay."

Dinah opened the door of the suite almost before Faith knocked, obviously as distressed as her companions. "I'm so glad you're here. I need to know these precious babies haven't been harmed beyond what we've already seen."

"Absolutely, Ms. Harper." Midge put a hand on Dinah's.

Dinah covered Midge's hand with her own. "Please call me Dinah. After all, it's your delicious cookies that our bunnies are enjoying, isn't it? Thank you for coming so quickly."

"All right, let's see how everyone is doing." With her trademark care, Midge examined each animal, murmuring softly as she did so.

Faith often thought Midge's consoling words and tone were just as much for the pets' owners as for the animals themselves. Her charming slight Southern accent seemed to add to the effect. She sounded calm and relaxed, and others tended to pick it up from her.

"Look at brave little Powder here," Midge said as she checked one rabbit. "He's holding his head up high despite what's happened. He may be small, but he's made of more than his fur. You take your cue from him, dear, and be brave too."

The owner nodded. "I will," she said tearfully. "He's just the best boy, isn't he?"

"Absolutely, and I see no nicks or cuts," Midge said as she gently turned the animal. She pointed to the uneven, choppy appearance of Powder's remaining fur. "I can tell you one thing. This wasn't done with an electric clipper. A pair of shears was used to remove this fur. With how unevenly it was cut, you might not be able to use the next shearing for yarn."

"As long as he's okay," the owner said. "And now we know the assault weapon at least."

"That's a bit drastic, don't you think?" Dinah cut in. "Powder is fine despite the theft of his coat."

"He most certainly is not," the owner said. "He's traumatized."

"We're all very upset," Francine said kindly.

Faith's admiration of the woman returned. In the time since the shearing, she'd regained her composure and done a marvelous job promoting calm despite the terrible loss of her own Beatrice's coat. If someone had harmed Watson in any way, Faith doubted she could show Francine's level of composure that quickly.

"Let's do as Dinah suggests and pull ourselves together," Francine went on even though her voice trembled. "No lasting harm has been done. Each of us has plenty of trophies already, and our bunnies will regrow their coats. We must remember that." She spoke as much to Beatrice as to the humans in the room. "Of course it's terrible now, but we are strong, aren't we?"

After assessing each of the rabbits and offering some advice on keeping them warm and healthy, Midge gave each owner an extra bag of the rabbit-friendly carrot cookies. "Just the thing for a hare's bad hair day," she joked.

Dinah gave a small laugh, but no one else did. "Thank you, Dr. Foster. We appreciate the care and the cookies."

"Everyone at the manor knows how to reach me if you need any further assistance," Midge said. "But in time your rabbits will be fine. Keep them warm and fed, and try to remain calm. They'll take their emotional cues from you. As Francine said, no permanent harm has been done. Y'all try to remember that, okay?"

"We will," Francine said. "Thank you."

"Gracious," Midge remarked as Faith shut the suite door behind them. "What a scene. But at least you have a few more clues to solve this crime."

Faith hadn't put that together until just now. "We do, don't we? Shears."

Midge nodded. "To use shears takes twice the time and effort of an electric clipper, but there'd be the advantage of no noise."

"Good point."

"Another thing I can tell you," Midge said. "Whoever did this knew exactly what they were doing. It takes time to shear a rabbit by hand, even if you're doing it sloppily. Plus, they didn't nick the skin at all. Angora rabbits have very delicate skin, and it's easy to nick it during a shearing and cause injury to the animal."

"So it was probably a rabbit owner or a breeder," Faith said.

"Definitely. Find who has those shears, and you'll find your culprit. Maybe spinning a whole bunch of new angora yarn."

"I'll keep my eyes out for shears or anything unusual," Faith said. "But there's already a lot that's unusual about this event."

Wolfe and Chief Garris met them at the bottom of the stairs to give them the results of the search.

"Nothing's missing from the pet spa," the chief announced.

"We're searching for shears," Faith said. "Midge says the rabbits weren't sheared with an electric clipper but by hand with shears."

"By someone who knew what he or she was doing," Midge added.

"The rabbits haven't been harmed, but they've been very effectively taken out of tomorrow's competition."

"There's your motive." Chief Garris pointed at Midge. "Now we need to figure out who had opportunity. How did someone get in and out of all three of those guest rooms unnoticed?"

"Let's go check with Marlene to see if any housekeeping keys have turned up missing," Wolfe suggested.

Marlene was a stickler about keys. She wore a set of manor keys on a large ring fixed to her waist like the grandest of Victorian house mistresses. If a master key had gone missing, she'd know. And so would everyone else.

Wolfe and the chief walked off in the direction of Marlene's office.

"Can you still make it to Snickerdoodles tomorrow?" Midge asked Faith.

She had almost forgotten about the coffee and dessert she'd planned with her friends for after the rabbit show. "I'm looking forward to it."

"I might be able to give you an answer about those white hairs by then," Midge went on. "I have to say, I'm 90 percent certain they're rabbit."

"No real surprise there," Faith replied. "The real question is, which rabbit?"

8

The cat stared at the strange sight in the back corner of the closet. He wasn't normally in the habit of inspecting guest room closets while guests were downstairs at dinner, but the scent of so many rabbits concentrated in this one spot was impossible to resist. Besides, with his extraordinary skills, he'd be in and out of the room with none of the humans the wiser.

Each rabbit in the manor smelled unique, but this one smelled like a mixture. There seemed to be only one ball of fur back there, but his nose told him there were several rabbits.

But the ball of fur did not move. Carefully, patiently, the cat waited for it to bolt or twitch or send up a pair of those silly long ears. He certainly wasn't going to provoke the thing. Still, it smelled so unusual. Suspicious, even.

With a start, the cat recognized the obvious detail he'd missed: the fur was in a plastic bag. No one, not even these strange humans and their outrageous rabbits, kept pets in plastic bags. Was it a stuffed rabbit?

With a bolt of clever feline deduction, the cat realized he was staring at neither animal nor stuffed toy. He was staring at a pile of rabbit fur. All fur, no animal. Piled up and stuck in the corner of this room's closet. Hidden.

Most of the other humans at the manor this week paraded their animals and piles of string and fur around like prizes. This was hidden, and that was important. This pile of fur was not meant to be found.

The cat knew that secrets do not stay hidden in a place like this with a cat of his talents around. Something was afoot—or rather, a-paw.

He'd need to give careful thought as to what this clue revealed. After all, it was his purpose to lend a paw when his human was unraveling a mystery.

And she would definitely need his help with this one.

Dinah's announcements at dinner had set the manor guests further abuzz. The earlier information that Maura's death had been classified as a murder was disturbing enough. The frightening details of what had now come to be known as "the vandalism shearing" simply made everything worse.

Was someone plotting ways to harm Dinah's career and disband her Bettys? Or were these unrelated incidents? While no one surprised Faith by taking credit for the sinister shearing, she was at least relieved that no one openly pointed fingers and accused another Betty.

"Dinah gave none of the details about Maura's murder," Wolfe remarked to Faith as they stood at the back of the room.

"That was smart," Faith replied. "It doesn't make sense to broadcast what the police know."

"I don't get the impression the police know much." Wolfe's frustration with the event's escalating stress couldn't be missed.

Everyone at the manor worried that things were spiraling out of control. Ron and Dinah were determined to press on, but how much more pressure could the group withstand?

"No, they don't know much," Faith said, "which makes any stray details that might surface more valuable. If someone lets some fact slip about Maura or how she was found, we'll know they didn't hear it from gossip."

Wolfe leaned against one of the dozen alabaster columns that gave the room such an elegant feel. "There's certainly enough of that going around."

Ron joined them. All the sleek executive appearance he'd shown on the first day was gone. "We made it through dinner. There's only dessert now. If we get through that without a scene, accusation, or incident, I'll be grateful." The poor man looked like he hadn't slept well since his arrival. "At least they'll have the contests tomorrow to keep them occupied."

"Do you really think it's a good idea to go on with the contests?" Wolfe asked. "Aren't things tense enough as it is?"

Ron nodded at Dinah, who stood with Francine and the other shearing victims, giving and receiving hugs from fans. "Dinah insists and I agree with her."

"Why?" Wolfe asked. "No offense to you and your event, but there are four more days, and it seems that things among the Bettys are getting out of hand."

How badly had things gotten out of hand between you and Maura? Faith wondered as she studied Ron. Garris had questioned the man about it and presumably been satisfied with his answers, whatever they were, so Faith saw little point in bringing that conflict up now.

She chose a different tactic instead by remarking, "I have to say I've been so impressed by Francine today. She's been such a voice of reason among the Bettys even while her own Beatrice was one of the victims."

"I think we've asked too much of Francine already," Ron replied. "I told her she ought to consider stepping down so she and Beatrice are less likely to be targets."

"Is that best?" Faith asked. "She seems determined to help, and you can certainly use her strong leadership right now."

"Francine is fantastic," Ron said, "but we'll find a way to get by without her. That bunny means the world to her. Pearl's offered to step in, and it'd be cruel not to let Francine take the time she needs to cope." His words were kind, but something in Faith's gut found them insincere.

"So you'll carry on," Wolfe said.

Ron sighed. "I don't see how we could do anything else. Things might get even more chaotic if we shut the event down now, and it would be a real shame to cancel the charity book signing. Besides, if Dinah says we keep on, then we keep on."

"Of course we're happy to host you," Wolfe said. "But I have to say, the possibility of some other attack happening seems to be fast outweighing the advantages."

"Believe me, I'm terribly upset by what's happened." Ron ran his hands down his face. "But this is a precarious point in Dinah's career. As awful as it is to consider, banding the Bettys together against a common threat—even one as terrible as this—could be a positive."

"Enough of a positive to offset all that's happened?" Wolfe pressed.

"Whether or not that's the case, Dinah believes that altering the event would feel like surrendering to whatever malicious person or group is trying to undermine things. And Dinah, very much like her Betty, never surrenders."

"That's admirable, but what if something else happens?" Faith felt compelled to ask. "We still don't know who pushed Maura off the balcony, and we still believe that person—whoever he or she may be—is likely here at the manor."

Dinah waved at Ron as a group of younger knitters approached Francine.

"Come over here," Ron said, motioning for Faith and Wolfe to join him. "You're going to want to see this. Dinah told me this was happening, and I think it will explain a lot of why she wants to continue."

As they walked toward the gathering, Faith watched the group of younger knitters hold up small sweaters in various states of progress.

"I don't know what to say," Francine said, her voice choked with emotion. "Thank you. It's so very sweet."

Dinah pulled Faith, Ron, and Wolfe into the conversation. "These young women have all decided to take themselves out of tomorrow's knitting competition and instead use their time, skills, and yarn to knit sweaters for the three bunnies who were attacked."

Angora sweaters for Angora bunnies? Faith beamed. It truly was a sweet thing to do.

"I've always suspected my fans are the best in the world," Dinah said, dabbing an eye, "but now I can say I know it for certain."

"Do you think Beatrice will like it?" Annette, the kind younger fan Faith had met earlier on the lawn—one who didn't even own a rabbit herself—held up her knitting needles upon which were the beginning rows of a soft mint-green garment.

"You had an impressive scarf already half-finished for the competition, didn't you?" Dinah said.

"Yes, but I can knit a scarf any old time," Annette said. "Right now I think it's more important to help out a fellow Betty and her rabbit."

Francine gave Annette a hug. "Thank you. Beatrice is sure to love it." She peered down at the young woman's name tag. "Annette? Have we met before? I can't help but think you look familiar."

"No, we've never met before this event," Annette said.

"Well, thank you." Francine seemed deeply moved.

"I was thinking Count Cotton was more of a stripes gentleman myself," a second young Betty said. "He'd want a dapper turtleneck." She held up a partially completed sweater with blue and white stripes.

Faith had to smile, thinking that Count Cotton might indeed end up being the best-dressed rabbit in the county.

"Several of the Bettys have given up their competition knitting," Ron said, sounding as proud and touched as Dinah. "Each of those rabbits is going to have a whole wardrobe of winter sweaters."

"Ronald, I've just had an idea," Dinah said.

Ron grinned at Wolfe. "When she says 'Ronald,' I've learned I should pretty much just give in and say yes right away, because she'll always win in the end."

"We're going to expand the knitting competition," Dinah declared.

"How?" Faith asked.

"We'll keep the old part where Bettys can knit up anything they want as long as it's with angora blends, but we'll add a special category just for bunny wear. I don't want the thoughtful fans who are knitting for Beatrice, Powder, and Count Cotton to lose their chance at prizes. Who knows? Maybe even more Bettys will decide to join and give those three even more sweaters."

"We couldn't do that," Francine protested.

"Why not?" Dinah said. "Bettys always help each other. I'll offer up a $250 cash prize myself." She turned to Ron. "Baxter House will match it for an even $500, won't you?"

Ron had been right in his assessment. Dinah's tone and expression gave no room for refusal.

"Wait," a woman from the table behind them said. "I can win $500 if I knit for the rabbits instead of making my mittens?"

"No, don't. It's too much," Francine protested.

"Oh, heavens, I disagree," Dinah said, putting an arm around Francine's shoulders. "It's not enough. This is a terrible trial. You and Beatrice deserve all the support we can give you."

Annette pulled out her phone. "I'll announce it over the group chat." She and her friends began tapping furiously on their phones, alerting other Bettys about this new element in the knitting competition.

"I'll go back up after dessert and make a formal announcement," Dinah said, then winked at Annette. "But I suspect everyone will know within the hour."

In fact, Faith saw Bettys already rushing around the room to spread the news.

"Look at my Bettys," Dinah boasted. "An unsinkable crowd, the lot of them."

Ron seemed like he wasn't quite sure what had just happened. "They're definitely something."

"It's because of you, Dinah," Francine said.

"No, I think it's because of Betty. She's the unsinkable heroine we all wish we could be. She's defended herself and those orphans from any number of dangers, and she never gives up." Dinah smiled at Faith. "Whenever I face a problem, I always find myself thinking, 'What would Betty do?'"

"That's exactly what I did," Annette piped up. "I had to do something, so I sat down and thought, 'What would Betty do?' And then I knew."

"My dear, that's the best thing an author could ever hear from a reader. And now look what you've made happen." Dinah took Francine's hand. "Let's go check on your darling Beatrice and let her know her wardrobe is about to grow by leaps and bounds. Or is that hops and bounds?"

Thursday's main events were the rabbit and knitting competitions. Ron was right. The excitement did seem to reenergize and focus the Bettys away from their fears and toward what they all shared. The manor was busy with Bettys furiously finishing their garments, grooming their bunnies, setting up displays, and chatting with one another.

The public was invited to the rabbit show, so of course Eileen and Midge came to see the spectacle. Brooke was too busy in the kitchen to attend.

"I've never seen anything like it." Eileen's face wore the same amazement Faith felt as they walked with Midge up and down the manor gallery.

Faith had to agree with her aunt. Down either side of the long hall, aisles of draped tables each held three or four rabbits in little cages or sitting on small squares of carpeting. Owners stood proudly behind their bunnies, talking with onlookers, answering questions, or combing the splendid coats.

Faith kept her eye out for any sign of shears, but she noticed only combs, brushes, and even hair dryers for blowing out loose fur. Every entry had a card at the front of the table listing the rabbit's name, its breed, and various other bits of information.

"It's like an encyclopedia of rabbits," Midge remarked.

"It's better than an encyclopedia of rabbits," Eileen marveled. "Look at the costumes!"

Indeed, some owners were dressed in clothing Faith guessed to be representative of the Betty Townsend novel era. One rabbit even stood next to an old-fashioned crank telephone, a nod to Betty's profession as a telephone operator. Many of the rabbit tables also displayed the ribbons and trophies the animals had earned in the past.

"I feel like I can't call them 'bunnies,'" Faith said. "These are the most immaculate and impressive rabbits I've ever seen."

"It's definitely as serious a competition as any pedigree dog or thoroughbred horse show I've ever attended," Midge said. "It's a wonder any of them have time to knit if they're tending to these coats."

"We make time for what we love, don't we?" Dinah asked, joining them. "Hello, Dr. Foster." She turned to Eileen. "You must be Faith's aunt. A knitter and a fan of Betty novels, so she tells me."

"Yes indeed." Eileen extended a hand. "It's a pleasure to meet you, Ms. Harper."

"Please call me Dinah," the author said warmly. She gestured around the hall. "They're extraordinary, aren't they?"

"They certainly are," Eileen agreed. "I mean, just look at this one." She motioned to a rabbit with a gray coat that seemed to fluff out to perfection in all directions. Except for the velvety black face, eyes, and twitching nose, anyone would be hard-pressed to realize there was a live animal under all that fur.

"That looks like two hours of grooming right there," Midge commented.

"Three and a half," the owner boasted. Her card listed her as Tricia Gordon. "And that's not counting the washing."

"Like I said, you make time for what you love," Dinah said. Her cell phone went off in her pocket, and she retrieved it, then scowled at the screen. "And for what you have to. Heavens, Ron's got something else he needs me to do." She returned her gaze to the group. "Would you ladies excuse me? Do enjoy yourselves."

"Love or not, I don't know how any of these owners finds time to—" Midge stopped midsentence, for in the time they'd turned away to chat with Dinah, the rabbit owner had resumed her knitting, stitching a pair of fuzzy mittens the exact color of the animal in front of her from yarn in a small bag slung over her shoulder.

"I have more trouble putting it down than I do finding time to do it," Tricia said in response to their astonished looks. She regarded her animal with clear affection. "It helps to have a never-ending supply of yarn handy too."

"You spin your rabbit's fur into yarn?" Faith asked.

"Straight from the source," the woman said. "Would you like to see how?"

"Yes," all three women said in unison.

Tricia produced another bag. "This is from her last shearing," she explained, showing them the fluff inside. Then she retrieved a gadget she called a drop spindle from inside the bag with the fur.

Working quickly and skillfully, Tricia spun the device and held a tuft of hair from the bag to the end of a long string of yarn coming from the spindle. As if it were nothing at all, she twisted and stretched the hair from the rabbit until it became yarn right in front of them.

"Look at that." Eileen's eyes were wide with admiration.

"It's faster when I use a spinning wheel, but it's not quite as portable." Tricia motioned to her rabbit. "Earl Grey's coat is lovely to work with."

"Who knew rabbits were so adorable, productive, and useful?" Faith remarked. "No wonder Watson seems to feel rather upstaged."

"Watson?" Tricia asked.

"I own a cat who often wanders the manor," Faith explained.

The owner gave a little start at the mention of a free-roaming feline among all these precious bunnies.

"A cat who's wise enough to stay at home today," Faith assured her, hoping it was true.

Faith had been as firm as she knew how in her command for Watson to stay at the cottage, and for once he seemed to have the good sense to obey her. Pulling one of his appearing tricks in the gallery or anywhere near it today might have caused an uproar from which the Bettys might not recover.

"Earl Grey really is beautiful," Eileen said, changing the subject. "And so is his fur and your knitting." She reached out to touch the silver-gray fuzzy mittens, oohing at their obvious softness.

"Thanks," Tricia replied. "With Earl Grey around and a Betty Townsend novel to read, I'm never bored. I look forward to this event every year. It's the highlight of my winter."

Tricia held the same expression of happiness and belonging that Faith had seen on so many other Bettys. No wonder Dinah was loath to even consider canceling the event or cutting it short. This was a true community.

Everyone deserves to have a place where they feel they fit right in, she thought. The camaraderie Dinah and Francine had built among the Bettys was an extraordinary thing indeed.

If someone felt that bond was under threat from Maura, that she failed to appreciate what the Bettys were to each other, would they go so far as to murder? Looking at the sweet face and disposition of the kindly woman knitting in front of her, it was hard to imagine.

"How long is Earl Grey's coat?" Midge asked.

"Seven inches," Tricia said proudly. "As of today, he probably has the longest coat here. I'll need to shear him as soon as we get home."

"As of today?" Eileen asked.

"Just the champion rabbits have longer coats," Tricia said. "I've always wanted to win but only if Beatrice or Lady Latte or one of the other champions retired. Not ever, ever because someone stole a glorious coat. It's shameful what's happened. I can't think anyone here would even be capable of such a thing."

"I have to agree," Eileen said. "It's like something right out of a Betty Townsend mystery."

"No it's not," Tricia replied. "Dinah would never put such a cruel act into one of her books. I can't believe it's happened. No one can. We're all heartsick for Francine and the others."

Faith had heard similar expressions of concern from any number of Bettys.

If the culprit of either crime—the murder or the shearing or both—was hiding among the Bettys, Faith was starting to worry whether he or she would ever be found.

9

By the time they'd walked down the full length of the gallery, Faith noticed Midge had grown quiet. "What's up?" she asked her friend. "Why do you seem so worried?"

Midge motioned Faith and Eileen farther into the corner and motioned toward Earl Grey. "It's what Tricia said."

"About always wanting to win but not by what happened to Beatrice or the others?" Faith asked.

"No, about the coat," Midge answered. "She said Earl Grey's coat was seven inches, and she thought the only rabbits with coats longer than that were the champions."

"I heard her," Faith said.

"The rabbit hair Chief Garris gave me to examine was seven and a half inches long." Midge paused. "And white."

Faith stared at her friend. "Only two rabbits have a coat like that."

"One of them doesn't have it anymore," Midge added.

"Meaning that it could only have been Beatrice's or Lady Latte's fur that was tangled in Maura's bracelet," Eileen said.

"Without getting some of both rabbits' hair for comparison, I can't say for certain," Midge admitted. "But I don't see any other explanation. Even so, why shear Beatrice and not Lady Latte?"

"From everything I've heard, Maura and Francine got along," Faith said. "Pearl doesn't seem to get along with anyone except Francine."

"So how did the hair get tangled in the bracelet?" Eileen asked.

"One of them must have been with Maura sometime shortly before she died." Faith gazed down the gallery to see Francine walking by the competitors she could no longer join. Francine's expression was full of sorrow. On the other hand, Pearl stood proudly behind Lady Latte. "Maybe one of them had an argument with Maura."

"Or worse," Midge said.

Faith checked her watch. "I'd better go. I don't want to be late for lunch. We'll meet up at Snickerdoodles later and talk about this more."

Wolfe had invited Faith to join him for lunch with Dinah and Ron as the rabbit show was concluding, so Faith hurried to the dining room.

"I wanted to make sure you felt things were under control and to see if there are any other ways we can help," Wolfe said as he pulled out a chair for Dinah.

"How thoughtful. Thank you." Dinah sighed as she sat down.

"How are you doing, Dinah?" Faith asked as she joined the others around the table. She had to admit, the author was showing signs of strain.

"I confess it's all getting to me," Dinah answered. "I still can't believe Maura is gone. Or that someone . . . took her from us."

Ron swallowed hard at Dinah's words. "We're pushing on as best we can, but it's been difficult."

"I'm sure it is. You'll be pleased to know that I heard a lot of the public saying they were very impressed with the event today," Wolfe said. "I think both your books and your Angoras earned a lot of new fans. I'm sure many of them will come back for the charity book signing too. I hope that's some comfort."

"Yes it is," Dinah replied.

"My friends were simply amazed at the rabbit show," Faith said. "Do you know which rabbits won the competition yet?"

Dinah and Ron exchanged meaningful glances.

"I'll formally tabulate the scores later, but Dinah tells me there will be some surprises at tomorrow night's awards dinner," Ron answered quietly.

"Honestly, I can't remember a contest where Francine's Beatrice didn't take one of the top three prizes," Dinah said as she placed her napkin on her lap.

"Francine did seem awfully sad today." Faith passed a basket of Brooke's delightful cinnamon bread. "It has to be very distressing for Beatrice to be taken out of the running like that."

"Frannie's made of strong stuff," Dinah said. "She'll pull through. So will Beatrice and the others, thanks to the darling efforts of those knitters. I'm looking forward to awarding those special prizes for the bunny sweaters."

"It's a first, that's for sure." Ron didn't sound very enthused as he passed the basket to Wolfe.

Dinah turned to Faith. "Did I tell you that one of my Bettys specializes in cat sweaters? She's asked to present one to your Watson as a thank-you for being so well-behaved with so many bunnies on the grounds this week."

"A sweater?" Faith asked in disbelief. "For Watson?" She tried to calculate how many tunaroons it would take to get her back in favor with her cat after something like that. By a conservative estimate, it would be . . . well, a lot.

Wolfe chuckled. "Now, there's a presentation I'd like to see."

Dinah raised an eyebrow at Wolfe. "You don't think Watson would like a sweater?"

"It's just that I've never seen a cat in a sweater," Wolfe replied diplomatically.

"Before this retreat, I'd never seen a rabbit in one either," Faith said, then smiled at Dinah. "That's a wonderful gesture. Thank you. I have to say, I've discovered your Bettys to be a lovely group of ladies."

"They are indeed," Ron said, filling his plate from the collection of delectable salads and sandwiches that were arranged at the center of the table. "And heaven knows we love how they buy and read Dinah's books."

"My aunt has loved your work for years," Faith told Dinah. "It was a delight to introduce her to you at the rabbit show today, and she's coming to the book signing too."

"Dinah has a rare way with fans, doesn't she?" Ron said with a smile.

"As I keep telling Ron, it isn't hard to like someone who enjoys books, knitting, and rabbits," Dinah said. "I always feel like every fan is an instant friend because we start out with so much in common."

"Eileen knits and loves your books," Faith said, "but so far she hasn't acquired an Angora bunny."

"What? Even after today?" Dinah teased. "I always find it hard not to come home with a new friend for Pouf if someone has a litter up for sale, and I saw notices for two litters today. Do tell your aunt that bunnies can be wonderful company. Or the Rabbit Rescue League will have dozens up for fostering after Easter, sad as that is. People adopt rabbits to give to their children for the holiday, but they don't take into account that rabbits are a responsibility and require care just like any other pet, so they surrender them pretty quickly thereafter."

"That is sad," Faith replied. "But Eileen is as busy as they come, so I suspect she's safe from temptation for now." Still, Eileen had traded in her average sedan for a red sports car not too many years ago, so Faith wouldn't put it past her aunt to suddenly take up rabbits in addition to her many hobbies and activities. "I met one Betty who didn't own a rabbit on the first day," she said, remembering Annette. "Are there many?"

"Not many and not for long." Dinah laughed. "I tease Ron that every Betty gets a bunny in the end."

"I think Dinah could write a grocery list, and they'd buy it up in a few weeks and demand a second printing," Ron said. Then he added, "I'm grateful Dinah isn't one to rest on her laurels. It's not every author who understands the need to stay relevant, to change with the times. Dinah does. This year will give Dinah the best of new fans and old, won't it?"

"That is the plan. But even best-selling authors need an editor, and now I don't have one," Dinah said with a tinge of sadness.

"Nonsense," Ron said, though he sounded more somber as well.

"You've got me. There was a time I was Baxter House's only editor, and I've worked closely with Claudia and Maura on your books. There's no reason I can't fill in while we find a replacement."

"Aren't you too busy?" Dinah asked.

"I'm never too busy for our best author," Ron reassured her.

"Well," Dinah said as she reached into her bag, "I suppose I should give you this." She handed Ron a three-inch stack of papers bound with red rubber bands.

"You finished your galleys? Here? With all that's going on?" Ron asked, surprise evident on his face.

Faith shared his astonishment. She'd had trouble concentrating on the index she'd been working on, and she wasn't nearly as embroiled in all the difficulties of the Betty event as Dinah was.

"I'm nothing if not a professional," Dinah said firmly. "If I'm honest, it's given me something to do in the middle of the night when I'm not sleeping well." The author looked at Faith and Wolfe. "Galleys are the final printouts of the book, how it will appear on the page when it's published. Every author signs off on her galleys."

"Not every author and certainly not one as established as yourself," Ron interjected. "It's a tedious task, and I've told Dinah she doesn't need to bother herself with it."

The author sighed. "I have to admit there are times when a tedious task is welcome."

Ron tucked the galleys into his briefcase and snapped it shut. "I trust everything was in order?"

"All but the strangest thing. The phone numbers were wrong."

Ron raised an eyebrow. "Phone numbers?"

"The exchanges. All those residences and businesses Betty patches through while she's at her switchboard. I keep a list of them." Dinah chose another sandwich from the serving platter. "Readers care about the smallest details, you know." She leveled a stare at Ron. "Several of them aren't the way I wrote them."

Ron frowned. "I'm sure that's not the case."

"Oh, I'm quite sure it is."

It was the first time Faith had heard even a hint of a sharp tone between them. Still, given the stress Dinah was under and the fact that she'd just admitted to not sleeping well, it was certainly understandable.

"More coffee, anyone?" Wolfe asked.

Faith appreciated how Wolfe tried to change the subject. The point of this luncheon had been to help things along, not ratchet up the tension. "Oh, I'd love some more. Thanks," she said.

Ron patted Dinah's hand. "I'm sure it's just a few typos. Nothing to be worried about."

"The readers won't be writing you to say I got the exchanges wrong," Dinah said. "They'll be writing me."

"They'll be writing you to say how much they love Betty's exciting new adventures and her thrilling romance," Ron replied.

Dinah aimed a resigned smile at Faith and Wolfe. "Ron's been in marketing as well as editing, as I'm sure you've gathered."

Ron spread his hands. "A publisher needs both. But what a publisher needs most of all is an author readers adore, and we've got that in spades with Dinah." He raised the coffee cup Wolfe had refilled. "I doubt there's another author in the country who could pull off what you've done here this week under such difficult circumstances. To you, Dinah."

"And to the Bettys," Dinah amended as she raised her cup.

Faith didn't find it hard to raise a cup in honor of both Dinah and her beloved Bettys.

"They made Watson a sweater?" Brooke's eyes were wide as everyone stared at the fuzzy yellow sweater Faith held up over their table of desserts at Snickerdoodles later that afternoon. "I'm glad I could sneak away to see this."

Aside from the library next door, Snickerdoodles Bakery & Tea Shop was their favorite place to meet for book discussions or social gatherings. Or mystery-solving brainstorming sessions.

"I think it's sweet," Faith said, determined not to sound ungrateful. "Atticus has a dozen sweaters, and everyone thinks they're adorable."

"Because they *are* adorable," Midge replied, "and Atticus enjoys being a well-dressed dog."

"Don't you think Watson wants to be a well-dressed cat?" Faith countered.

Brooke smirked. "I think Watson already considers himself a well-dressed cat."

"I've never met a tuxedo cat who acts more like he's actually in a tuxedo," Midge joked. "Watson might consider a sweater a downgrade. And some cats don't like wearing clothes. I think it feels too restrictive."

"Then there's the whole cats-and-yarn thing," Brooke added, staring at the sweater. "I don't know . . ."

Faith straightened. "Well, I do know that this was a thoughtful gesture on the part of the Bettys, and I think Watson should welcome a bit of extra style."

"Make sure you let us know how the first try-on turns out," Eileen said with a grin. "We'll want photos."

Brooke and Midge enthusiastically agreed that a photo of Watson wearing the sweater would be a prize indeed.

"So how did your lunch with Dinah go?" Eileen asked.

"It was difficult," Faith admitted.

"Difficult?" Midge asked. "Why?"

"Wolfe and I ended up sitting through a bit of an argument between Ron and Dinah. Nothing huge, just something editorial over details in her book. Actually, they were phone numbers."

"Betty is a telephone operator, after all," Brooke said. "There were lots of those in her book. I found it rather interesting. Phones were so different than they are these days."

"What was wrong with the phone numbers?" Midge asked.

"Was Dinah upset that they weren't consistent?" Eileen asked.

"Yes, that's exactly it. How did you know?" Faith replied.

"I've caught that exact mistake in the last two books," Eileen said. "In fact, I'm a little surprised that mistake happened again. I can't be the only one who noticed."

"You keep track of the phone numbers in Betty Townsend books?" Brooke asked. It was hard to tell if she was impressed or concerned.

"Only one. The phone exchange for the bank is my birthday. Or was, up until two books ago. It's been different in each of the last books. Just a digit or two each time but definitely off. I'd be upset at a mistake like that if I were Dinah. Her research is usually top-notch. It's one of the reasons I like her so much."

"She was upset," Faith confirmed. "Ron pretty much brushed it off, but I felt Dinah was right to be annoyed if no one caught it."

"It seems an easy detail to get right," Midge added. "Not to speak ill of the dead, but isn't that what editors are for?"

"Ron volunteered to serve as Dinah's editor until they replace Maura," Faith said.

"Ron, who doesn't care about the little details that are so important. At such a crucial time in her career." Eileen sighed and broke off a chunk of the brownie she'd selected. "It doesn't seem fair to Dinah. I may go ahead and join the Bettys as a show of support."

"You'd fit right in," Faith replied. "All you need is a bunny."

"I don't have the time to take care of one," Eileen said. "Did she tell you who's winning the top prizes tomorrow night?"

"Just a hint that some might be going to newcomers," Faith said.

"Poor Francine. It must have hurt her not to be in the competition," Eileen remarked. "So, who do you all think will take first place?"

"I'd have to say Pearl Quinton's rabbit, Lady Latte," Faith guessed.

"She's the vice president of the Bettys, isn't she?" Midge asked.

"Yes, and I worry that Pearl won't be especially gracious about winning. She seemed rather smug at the rabbit show. According to Dinah, she has waited a long time to take the top podium."

"Tired of losing to the longtime champion, eh?" Brooke asked suspiciously. "Maybe tired enough to do something drastic?"

"Could be," Faith said. "She's not a nice woman, but going so far as to shear the coat of her friend's rabbit in order to win? It's a bit of a stretch from not nice to outright cruel like that. Besides, she loves rabbits. I don't think she'd do anything to one of them."

"Even if she did, it doesn't get us any closer to solving who pushed Maura to her death," Brooke pointed out.

"Actually, it might," Midge said. "Pearl's rabbit, Lady Latte, is white and brown. With long fur. Long enough for the white fur to match the hairs found in Maura's bracelet."

"But why?" Eileen asked. "Why would Pearl want to kill Maura?"

"What if Maura wouldn't give her what she wanted?" Faith responded. "What if Pearl wants to take Francine off the top podium in more than just one place—as president of the Bettys?"

"Wouldn't that be Dinah's decision, not Maura's?" Eileen asked.

"I'd think funding for Betty events and such has to come from Baxter House, so maybe it is a publisher decision," Faith said. "I did hear Ron say Pearl is willing to step in if Francine was too upset to lead the group."

"So she does have designs on leading the group," Brooke said.

"Either way, Maura didn't strike me as a big fan of the Bettys," Faith said. "I think she felt fan clubs were old-fashioned."

"So if Pearl came to Maura to put herself forth as the next president, Maura might have shut her down and admitted she was in favor of dissolving the Bettys," Eileen concluded.

Faith could imagine the sour woman's reaction. "That would be a battle for sure."

"Which means Pearl could be our killer," Brooke said. "And our shearer."

"Perhaps," Faith agreed. "But it's still only a theory until we can prove it."

W*hat* on earth was his human holding?

She came toward him with a ghastly ball of fuzzy fabric in a horrifically bright color. The cat knew that a ball of yarn could be great entertainment, but this was not in fun string form.

It was made of rabbit fur. Not only were there balls of rabbit fur in manor closets, but now there was one in his own house. With horror, he realized what it was.

His human held up the monstrosity as though he should be thrilled to have such a thing anywhere near him. "Look at the little buttons, Rumpy. I won't even have to pull it over your head."

Pull it over my head? As in put it on? What am I, the vet's little dog? He shrank back in disgust as his human held up the open thing to show him holes where his legs would go. He'd seen such ridiculousness on dogs too witless to know they didn't have to stand for such a disgrace. His fur was more than sufficient, thank you.

"It's the very height in handmade feline fashions," his human coaxed.

Nothing anywhere justified the existence of feline fashions. Handmade or otherwise.

Obviously mistaking his revulsion for shyness, she plucked him off the carpet before he could escape.

It felt like he was being clothed in the plastic bag he'd seen in the manor closet.

And worse yet—the color! The cat could think for five years and not dream up a greater indignity for any self-respecting feline.

"Now just hold still. This won't take a moment." She tugged his paws through the holes for them.

The cat focused on every reason he loved his human and trusted her judgment.

Before he could howl loudly enough to show his growing displeasure, she began fastening the little fish-shaped buttons down his back.

He was wearing a sweater. A rabbit sweater with fish buttons. He had never endured such disgrace. It itched. It was hot. It was made from something that should be his dinner, not his wardrobe. He actually would have preferred to wear the plastic bag he'd found earlier. That object could at least be an important clue. This was nothing less than humiliating.

"There, see? It's not so bad," his human cooed. Then she reached for her cell phone and began snapping photos. "It's actually kind of cute. The girls will love this."

It's abominable, he thought, pawing unsuccessfully at the itchy thing. Could he duck through thorns and snag the thing beyond repair? Rub up against a garden rake? Run to some other sensible human and beg for mercy? He resisted the urge to try to back out of the sweater, knowing it would be no use.

He'd always thought his human was of the sensible variety, but clearly all those silly women with their overcoiffed bunnies and their pointy sticks had addled her brain.

She grinned at him. "Don't you love it?"

He possessed a perfectly lovely coat that made him appear dignified. Now it was covered by a sweater that made him look like a walking fuzzy lemon. He wanted this thing off immediately.

He twitched his tail in a way sure to let his human know his intense displeasure. He narrowed his eyes and did everything but hiss. He would never, ever hiss at her, but then again she'd never done anything so mortifying.

"And guess what?" she continued. "You'll have two more by the end of this event. Those Bettys are so generous. Knitting sweaters for you. Imagine."

They were neither kind nor generous. They had infested the manor with rabbits. And now they had put clothing on him. The cat was inclined

*to think those humans were among the worst, most intolerable ones he'd
ever met.*

"Oh," his person added, reaching for the kitchen counter, "one of them
found out how much you like tunaroons and brought you some." She held
out no less than four of the delectable morsels.

Well, maybe not the worst humans he'd ever met.

Maybe just somewhere in the top five.

While any day could be busy or quiet in the library, Fridays in
other parts of the manor—especially the kitchen with tonight's Betty
Townsend awards dinner—could feel hectic.

Faith had a productive couple of hours, then went to Iris for a
midmorning coffee break. Her pleasant chat with Iris was interrupted
by an irritated Marlene. Even more so than usual.

"I never," Marlene grumbled as she barked an order for a cup
of tea and a muffin. She impatiently rearranged Iris's mug display
while she waited. "It's bad enough one of the housekeepers lost her
key for half a day. But those rabbits. I thought I'd seen it all from
those beasts."

"Something new go wrong?" Faith hadn't heard any reports
of rabbit destruction other than excessive amounts of shed hairs
putting a strain on the housekeeping vacuums. In fact, most
reports from all manner of staff had categorized the bunnies as a
well-behaved bunch.

"And here I thought their chewing would do the most damage to
manor property," Marlene groused. "It's a wonder you've been spared.
I'd like to prohibit rabbits from the entire estate."

"I know this has been taxing for you." Faith had opted to play it
on the safe side and declare the library off-limits to bunny-kind, both

for the books and in an attempt to give Watson at least one safe haven should he disobey orders and show up again. She braced herself before asking, "Why don't you tell me what's happened?"

"Now some of the rabbits are lethargic," Marlene said. "Their owners are sick with worry."

"Oh no. Poor little bunnies."

Marlene huffed. "I wouldn't be surprised if it's all those cookies they're eating. Every day those beasts get another bag of cookies."

Faith could imagine how upsetting the addition of a rabbit epidemic to the recent series of misfortunes would be for this crowd. She suspected her friend's cookies weren't the cause. "Midge would never give those rabbits something that wasn't good for them. She's too careful about her ingredients. Did you call her to examine the rabbits?"

"Of course," Marlene snapped back. "It was the first thing I did. Our animal baker," she said, using the term without any kindness, "should be here in ten minutes." She took the tea and muffin Iris handed her and grumbled.

"You know, it might not be the cookies," Faith suggested. "So many animals together that aren't regularly with other rabbits—"

"A rabbit virus?" Marlene nearly yelped. "That's the absolute last thing we need on top of everything else that's happened. This whole event has been nothing short of a catastrophe."

"Well then, it's a blessing Midge is not only a baker but a veterinarian. Besides, not every bunny is lethargic, right?" Faith said, trying to insert some calming bit of news.

"Only half a dozen, but it's made all the guests panicked. Well, *more* panicked. They're worried it's a new attack by the vandalism shearer." Marlene snorted derisively.

"The vandalism shearer?" Iris appeared baffled and only slightly less so after Faith explained the mysteriously sheared rabbits.

Betty Townsend Week really was coming to defy rational descriptions. It surely was pushing Marlene to the limits of her tolerance for the manor's nonhuman guests. And likely many of their human guests as well.

Faith walked back to the library and tried to keep to her tasks of guest research and intake of a few new books that had arrived. It didn't work. She found herself too worried about the fate of the listless rabbits. It seemed unfair that kind Dinah and her friendly Bettys had had their event marred by so much trauma.

"Sorry for your emergency house call," Faith said when Midge stopped by the library to give her an update an hour later. "And for Marlene's suspicion of your cookies."

"Oh, she's made no secret of how she suspects my treats." The veterinarian put down her bag and planted her hands on her hips. "Not that she believes me when I tell her it isn't the cookies."

"What's really wrong with the bunnies?"

"I can't be certain, but there's no evidence that the cookies are to blame." Midge sat down in front of Faith's desk, clearly grateful for the quiet peace of the library. "I'm glad Dinah refused to cancel tomorrow and Sunday's cookie deliveries. Not that Marlene didn't suggest it. I think those bunnies are lethargic because of the stress of being in a new environment."

"That makes sense," Faith said. "I wouldn't imagine that rabbits are the best travelers."

"It's true," Midge agreed. "But I did find something odd in their hutches. Well, I'd say it's odd, but there's been too much about this whole event that's odd."

"What did you find?"

Midge produced a plastic bag from her medical satchel and held it up. It contained two or three sections of typewritten pages. "I asked all the owners if they'd put the paper in the hutches, but none of them had."

"Who else would do it?" Faith asked.

"That's a good question, but the real question is, what were the papers originally?" Midge handed the bag to Faith. "Any chance you can make sense of what these are?"

"As in what kind of papers?" Faith studied them, but they seemed to be ordinary typewritten pages to her.

"Look closely," Midge said. "They're not pages out of a book, but they're definitely some kind of text that's been marked up. See the handwriting?"

Faith squinted at the scraps of paper. Each scrap not only contained typing but marks of red handwriting. "I do. It's editing, I'd say."

"That was my guess too," Midge continued, pointing to a corner of one page. "Especially since the name *Betty* is on several of them."

Were they Betty Townsend manuscript pages? Faith gasped when she recognized them—from yesterday's luncheon. "These are from the manuscript Dinah gave Ron. Or one just like it." She stared at Midge. "Who would put a Betty Townsend manuscript in rabbit hutches? Especially here?"

"That's what I'd like to know," Midge said.

Faith flattened one of the sections out. A leaden ball of dread settled into her stomach as she realized what had to be the reason. "I think someone was trying to get rid of the pages. And here's why," she said as she pointed to a specific piece of text. "Do you see what that is?"

"Numbers?"

"Not just any numbers. That's a telephone exchange from the Betty Townsend era. And see there? Dinah marked it in red to change it back from however it had been altered." Faith peered more closely at one of the other sections Midge had saved. "Those numbers have been marked by Dinah as well. I don't know that I'd recognize her handwriting, but it looks just like the manuscript she handed back to Ron at lunch."

Midge examined the bag. "But there wasn't a whole manuscript's worth of pages in the hutches I saw. If Ron wanted to destroy Dinah's changes, why get rid of only some of the pages?"

"The only explanation is that Ron wanted the phone number alterations—and only those—gone."

Midge sat back. "Why disregard those corrections but keep the others?"

"I have no idea, and I doubt he'd tell us if we asked him." Faith tapped a finger against her chin. "I think he's hiding something, and it has to do with why the phone numbers are changed in Dinah's books."

This was shaping up to be a mystery worthy of the Candle House Book Club's combined sleuthing talents. Or maybe even Betty Townsend.

"Can we ask Dinah?"

"It doesn't sound like she knew anything about when it happened or why." Faith snapped her fingers as something clicked. "But Maura might have. I heard her and Ron arguing the first day they arrived, and it could have been about this. What if she found the changes and confronted Ron about them?"

Midge gulped. "That means Ron would have motive to kill Maura over whatever they were." She glanced up at the balcony. "He's definitely strong enough to push a small woman like her over the balcony edge."

Faith followed Midge's gaze. An icy tingle ran down her spine as the unwelcome vision of Maura's fall at the hands of Ron Powers leaped into her imagination. His words in the stairwell had been fierce enough, as had Maura's. "I hate to say it, but it seems easier to imagine Ron killing Maura for some professional reason than it is to picture one of the Bettys as a murderer."

"The Bettys are sweet. I mean, they knit sweaters for cats. Loved the photo, by the way." Midge laughed. "I can't believe Watson actually consented to wearing a sweater."

"I think he's just tolerating it for my sake." She opened her desk drawer and pulled out the second and third sweaters Annette and her friends had delivered that morning. "He'll never forgive me, but at least he'll be the best-dressed cat in town."

"He might be the only dressed cat in town." Midge smiled. "Maybe I should bring Atticus to the manor before they all leave. Or get them to share their patterns with Eileen. I've been meaning to ask her if she'd consider knitting something for him."

"You know Eileen. I'm sure she would. She loves a yarn-related challenge."

"So where is the best-dressed cat in Lighthouse Bay this morning?" Midge asked. "I'd love to see him in person."

"He's hiding out in the cottage today," Faith answered. "He'll put up with a sweater but not in public."

"Best for everyone, bunnies included," Midge said. She motioned toward the bag of page pieces. "Do you think I should take these over to Chief Garris? I've handled them, but they might be evidence."

"Garris told me he'll be back here this afternoon. I can turn them over if you'd like."

"That will work for me. I'll probably be back tomorrow to check on the rabbits' improvement. I've told Marlene the worst is over, but I'm not sure she believed me."

Faith laughed. "Marlene won't believe the worst is over until all the rabbits are on that bus and heading down the drive."

Midge grinned. "I believe it. Well, good luck with the awards dinner. It's great that Wolfe invited you when they included him. Who doesn't like a nice night out?"

Faith raised an eyebrow. "Somehow I don't think this qualifies as a nice night out. Tonight will probably feel more like keeping the peace."

"You'll have the most charming bachelor in Lighthouse Bay on your arm," Midge said, winking. "I think you'll find a way to make the most of it." She picked up her veterinary bag. "I'll expect a full report tomorrow. On you and Watson both, come to think of it."

"Yes, Dr. Midge." Faith gave her friend a cheerful salute.

Faith had another visitor when Brooke walked in a little while later to say hello as well. "I came by to get a peek at the cat in the sweater. And his librarian," she teased. "Where is the fancy fellow?"

"He's home today," Faith replied.

"I also came to say I take it all back," Brooke said, waving a small knitted item in her hand.

"Take what back?"

Brooke held up the object with a smile. "All my remarks about Watson and sweaters from the Bettys. They're thoughtful women. Look at this." She handed the item to Faith.

It was roundish, like a swollen hat, but with a clever wave design knitted into the sparkly ribbed fabric. "A cozy for your teapot?" Faith guessed.

"Better," Brooke replied. "It's a bowl cozy."

"For ice cream?" Faith asked. Then she hit upon the reason for Brooke's wide smile. "For Diva and Bling?"

Brooke's eyes sparkled. "Isn't it adorable? I didn't even know there was such a thing as a fishbowl cozy."

"It doesn't seem very practical," Faith said dubiously as she returned the cozy to her friend.

"As practical as a sweater for a cat. Or a rabbit," Brooke said. "It's decorative and protective. They spend most of their time in the tank, but they use a bowl when I'm cleaning their tank or when they travel. They might even want to come to book club meetings if they were snuggled in this, don't you think?"

"Do they like it?" Faith was momentarily struck by the absurd nature of asking whether two fish would enjoy a hand-knit fishbowl cozy. Then again, she'd been asking scores of questions this week that she'd have previously considered absurd.

"They love it." Brooke turned the cozy this way and that, admiring it. There was no mistaking the joy in her eyes at receiving the gift. "Of course they can't see out when it's on their bowl, but I think they find it rather snug. Everyone likes a bit of privacy from time to time."

Brooke had always been convinced that Diva and Bling had extraordinary powers of emotional perception, usually mirroring whatever Brooke was thinking or feeling.

"It's the sweetest gift, isn't it?" Brooke went on. "I'm sorry I said anything about Watson's sweater. How could he not love something given with such a generous spirit?"

"The Bettys are so kind and talented," Faith said.

"Well, it's my talents that are in demand tonight, so I'd better get back to work."

As Faith walked her friend to the door, a staff member delivered a package from one of the book repair companies where she'd sent two of the volumes damaged in Maura's fall. Each completed repair felt as if it nudged the library back to its former peace and quiet.

Faith glanced up at the balcony as she carried the package to her desk. *We'll figure out what happened to you, Maura. I promise.*

11

The cat had tried several schemes to escape the confines of the fuzzy monstrosity, but no matter how much he pulled or squirmed or yanked, the confounded thing wouldn't come off his back. The fluffy yarn tickled his whiskers. It made him hot, and the reflection of himself he'd seen in the bedroom mirror made him never want to leave the cottage again.

Knowing his only hope was to have someone stop by the house and save him, the cat was relieved to hear his human talk about the nice man from the manor coming over. Surely another male would understand why this sweater was a supremely bad idea.

When the doorbell rang, the cat bounded to the door ahead of his human, eager to make a connection and arrange his rescue.

When the nice man walked into the cottage, the cat knew he had an ally. The human clearly recognized the wrong that had been done. Sympathy filled the man's eyes as he looked down at the cat and said with an appropriate level of shock, "Watson is wearing a sweater."

The cat silently begged him to do something about it.

"Isn't it adorable?" his human said. "The Bettys made him three of them."

There were more? How could she not have realized the error of her ways? No matter how he had stared at her, she hadn't removed the offending garment. Even his protest of refusing to leave the house dressed like this seemed to go unnoticed. She obviously loved her own fancy outfit, and somehow she seemed to think the yellow atrocity gave him the same pleasure her finery gave her.

Cats were not meant to dress up. Only dogs could be expected to submit to that kind of humiliation.

At least the man seemed to understand. He wore a dignified tuxedo, *which only made the cat feel more ridiculous. His own glorious tuxedo was shamefully covered.*

"It's very . . . yellow," the man said diplomatically.

The cat pawed furiously at the thing.

"Are you sure he's not too warm?" the man called out while his human was in the bedroom fussing with something. "Maybe we should take it off him while you're out. You know, so he doesn't ruin it or something."

The cat arched his back toward the man, showing him exactly where the buttons that would lead to his freedom were located.

"I don't think she heard me." The man smiled down at him. "Let's get you out of this thing anyway, shall we?"

Success!

But before the man could rescue him, his human called from the other room, "While I get my bag, can you check the lock on my front door with your master key? My key's been sticking a bit lately. That way I can tell Mack that it's my key and not the lock that needs fixing."

"Certainly. We need your locks working well at all times." The man abandoned his mission of mercy and instead went to fiddle with the front door.

This was not at all what the cat wanted. He needed the man to remove the sweater, not be distracted by doing favors for his human.

The cat bounded over to where the man was inspecting the lock.

"My key seems to work fine," the man said. "Have Mack replace yours with—hey!"

In a burst of brilliant attention-getting strategy, the cat had brushed up against the man's dark pant leg, leaving a trail of yellow fuzz. Surely this would show the man how irritating the sweater was and why it needed to be removed immediately.

His human returned to the room, then gasped and pointed to the yellow fuzz now on the man's pant leg. "Oh, now look at you. I'll go get my lint brush to clean you up, and then we'd better get going."

The cat pushed up against the man's leg again, leaving more fuzz. If the nice man left this house without getting this abominable thing off him, he didn't know what he'd do.

"I got the message, and I'm with you," *the man said when she'd left the room.* "Sweaters belong on—well, not on cats."

The cat purred with relief as he felt the man's fingers release the dreadful buttons. He was free! The thing was off.

"You owe me," *the man said with a wink.*

The cat agreed.

"Oh," *his human said as she returned to the room.* "You took it off him." *Did she sound disappointed? The traitor.*

The man shrugged. "He was going to get us both all fuzzy."

The cat meowed in agreement. He would happily have covered both of them if it meant being released from the fluffy prison.

His human handed the brush to the man, and the cat watched as she folded the awful thing and placed it on the couch. "I mean, the Bettys worked so hard, and it was such a nice gesture."

Good. It was within his reach. The only thing he had to do now was shred it to pieces before she returned.

"Welcome to the Betty Townsend Week Fan Awards Dinner," Ron said from the podium. "I know this has been a difficult few days for many of us, but in true Betty fashion, we've persevered. Give yourselves a round of applause, and then we've got quite a few important announcements to make."

The crowd clapped.

"I was hoping we'd be able to announce that Maura's killer had been brought to justice tonight," Wolfe confessed to Faith as the applause died down.

"I know. Me too," Faith replied, taking in Dinah's drawn and tired face.

Dinah stood next to Ron at the podium. She was keeping up a brave front, but even Faith could see she'd been worn down by all the trauma and tension. Things were civil between her and Ron during the meal, but the edge that had appeared at lunch the previous day was still present. Clearly, all was not well between the author and her publisher.

"Ladies and gentlemen, I give you the reason we are all here—the incredible Ms. Dinah Harper." Ron gestured at Dinah, then took a seat.

Enthusiastic clapping and cheers filled the room.

Dinah smiled at her fans. "It has been an extraordinary week indeed, and we've been privileged to see some of the finest specimens of Angora rabbits anywhere."

The audience applauded again.

"I know what you are all waiting for, so let's get right to the rabbit show awards," Dinah continued. "I must say, I can't remember a year when the judging was more difficult for Ron and me."

"I swear she says that every year," Pearl muttered. She sat on the other side of the table.

"Maybe because it's true," Francine replied soothingly. "I expect it was even harder this year with some of the regular winners taken out of the running."

"Well, yes, of course," Pearl conceded.

Faith thought the strain between these two friends seemed as strong as the one between Ron and Dinah.

"In third place, we have a newcomer to the Betty ranks, Miss Charlotte Hanover and her lovely Clover."

Shouts of victory erupted from a table of younger Bettys off to one side of the room.

A young woman bounded up to the stage to accept her award. She even snapped a photo with Dinah before returning to her seat, something that made Pearl groan.

"In second place, a longtime favorite of the Betty community, Tricia Gordon and Earl Grey."

"She showed us how she spins Earl Grey's gorgeous fur into even more gorgeous yarn," Faith explained to Wolfe. "It was amazing."

The older Bettys applauded especially loudly as Tricia accepted her ribbon from Dinah.

Faith watched Francine and Pearl brace themselves for the announcement of the blue ribbon. The reactions of the two women couldn't have been more different.

Francine's shoulders sagged as she stared at her hands folded in her lap.

Poor thing. This must be so hard for her.

Pearl, on the other hand, watched Dinah with bright eyes. She clearly expected best in show to go to Lady Latte.

"And now," Dinah said from the podium, "I'm delighted to present our highest prize. First place goes to none other than Pearl Quinton and the beautiful Lady Latte, with seven glorious inches of divine fur."

Pearl stood with great ceremony, basking in the applause that rang out with an expression of triumph. Without even so much as a backward glance at the crushed Francine, Pearl strode to the stage to accept the top honor.

Francine clapped with everyone else, but her eyes were sad.

Faith quickly pulled out her phone.

"What are you doing?" Wolfe asked.

"Texting Midge," Faith said. She tapped out a message to her friend: *Lady Latte's fur is seven inches.* Lowering her voice so no one else would hear, she added, "We think the length of Lady Latte's fur could be a clue to the murder."

Wolfe nodded. "The bracelet?"

He said it a little too loudly because Francine's gaze snapped to them. "What bracelet?"

"One the color of Pearl's dress that's on sale in our gift shop," Faith improvised. "I should show it to Pearl before she leaves. It would go so nicely." She smiled, hoping the conversation about that crucial murder scene detail would end there.

Francine was taking a breath to ask another question, but Pearl's return to the table intervened.

"The blue ribbon!" Pearl crowed. "I know you've got loads of these, Frannie, but I must say I am pleased to finally have one of my own."

"Congratulations," Francine managed, still not looking her friend in the eye. "Lady Latte has always been a lovely bunny." Her words were kind, but the tone was flat and sad.

Faith cringed. Things were feeling decidedly frosty between the two Bettys. They'd appeared to be longtime friends at the beginning of the week, but Faith found herself wondering if the friendship would survive the event.

"Let's applaud all our winners," Dinah urged. "And remember to show our support of those poor rabbits taken out of competition. They and their owners are heroes and heroines, one and all." She led the room in a rousing surge of applause.

Pearl smiled. "These awards are proof again of what I always say—Bettys breed a better brand of bunny."

"The best brand of bunny," Francine said under her breath, "until they're vandalized."

"Try not to be so sour," Pearl admonished. "Like you said, Beatrice will grow her fur back. Maybe better than ever." With that, she turned to accept the congratulations of another Betty who had come over to the table.

Touched by the sad tint of the elegant woman's eyes, Faith felt compelled to recognize Francine's difficult situation. "I really am so very sorry for what happened to Beatrice."

Francine sighed. "I don't know what the world is coming to when you can't have a nice vacation with your pet and your friends."

"Don't be silly," Pearl said as she turned back toward the table. "There's still the knitting competition, and you're bound to take home a ribbon there."

"Of course, we all know that tonight is about more than just bunnies," Dinah continued from the podium as if she'd overheard. "We also celebrate the astounding creativity of Betty Townsend fans." She swept her hand toward the banquet room wall. "Take a look at that stunning needlework."

A set of ribbons had been strung across the wall like brightly colored clotheslines, and each knitting entry had been hung from the lines so that the wall had been transformed into an impressive display of knitted finery. There were hats and shawls, mittens and baby blankets, socks, and even several sweaters—all from a rainbow of fluffy angora yarn. Another line displayed an inventive collection of rabbit sweaters knit for the sheared Angoras.

Seeing the spectacular creations, Faith was suddenly inspired to give knitting another try or at least find an art form where she could contribute some kind of beauty to the world.

"Despite all the difficulties," she whispered to Wolfe, "I think the Bettys have become one of my favorite groups of guests. Maybe we can have them back next year."

"To enjoy a perfectly peaceful event next time. Do you think it's possible?" Wolfe mused.

"Anything's possible," Faith replied.

"And don't forget," Dinah continued from her place onstage. "Tonight we add a selection of rabbit-size sweaters in their own competition. Another display of Betty compassion and resourcefulness. I truly do have the best fans in the world."

Ron rejoined her at the podium. "Before we award those coveted prizes, I have an announcement that's sure to make all you Bettys feel like winners. It comes as no surprise to you that Betty Townsend's new adventures have met with tremendous success."

"Well, it's news to me, that's for sure," Pearl griped, not bothering to keep her voice down.

"What you don't know is that the new style of Betty novels will not only grace your bookshelves but your television screens as well," Ron said. "You are the first to find out that the LitChannel has optioned the next four Betty Townsend novels as a television series." He smiled and clapped enthusiastically.

Faith couldn't help but notice Dinah's enthusiasm didn't quite match her publisher's.

Pearl spun around to Francine. "The LitChannel? Did you know about this?"

"I'm still president, so I might have heard something," Francine said, clapping politely and raising her chin. She seemed a bit proud to have scooped her friend on such important news.

Response to the announcement was clearly mixed. The younger Bettys cheered and clapped, but the older ones frowned and muttered to each other.

Pearl glared at Francine. "As president, I hope you told Dinah what a terrible idea that is. The LitChannel? They're the people who did that hideous adaptation of *Little Women*. The costumes were completely inauthentic, and it didn't follow the book at all. They'll ruin Betty."

"I don't think Dinah would let them," Francine said. Faith didn't think she sounded convinced.

"Look at her," Pearl countered. "I don't think Dinah had any say in this. It's all Ron's doing. Or Maura Webber. I've always said it would be the beginning of the end when Claudia left."

Faith found it rather reckless of Pearl to come on so strongly as an opponent of Maura, given that the murderer had yet to be found. Still, as she glanced around the room, it was clear Pearl had company in her skepticism.

The exact opposite reaction radiated from the table where Annette and her friends were sitting. The younger Bettys happened to be right behind where Faith and Wolfe were seated, and they buzzed with excitement. In fact, Annette was already tapping away on her phone, probably sharing the news.

"Betty on television," one young woman said to another.

"Can you imagine?" another woman said. "I can't wait to see who they cast as Betty."

Francine said nothing, and Pearl rolled her eyes.

"Never mind that," another fan said. "Which hunk will they cast as Lieutenant Drake?"

That remark earned groans of annoyance from both Francine and Pearl. At least they'd found one point of agreement.

"I'm glad Claudia's not around to see this," Francine said. Her tone was sadder than Pearl's unchecked resentment. "I think it would break her heart."

"They should bring her back," Pearl snapped. "She'd never have let Dinah be railroaded like this. LitChannel indeed. They won't come close to doing it justice. I'm sure this was likely Maura's doing. I'm not afraid to say it—I'm glad she's gone."

Wolfe caught Faith's eye. If she'd hinted by her text to Midge that the book club considered Pearl a suspect, his expression said he agreed.

"With that happy news shared," Ron called loudly into the microphone in an attempt to bring the room's commotion back under control, "let's get on with the awards for needlework."

"You know you're sure to win this," Pearl said, squeezing Francine's arm. "You deserve it. After all, you had the rabbit championship stolen from you."

Faith couldn't help but wonder if it had been Pearl who had done the stealing. Everything the woman said tonight seemed to paint her in a more suspicious light.

"It would be nice," Francine replied. "But Dinah's not supposed to bias her awards."

"She wouldn't need to," Pearl said. "Everyone knows your shawls are in a totally different league than anything the rest of us could do."

Ron cleared his throat. "Third place in the general division—since we have a special rabbit division this year—goes to Gloria Thompson for her exquisite mittens."

A spotlight landed on a pair of truly beautiful white furry mittens mounted on the wall.

A woman from the far corner of the room squealed in delight and rushed to the stage to accept the ribbon Dinah handed to her.

"Second place goes to our beloved Francine Nelson," Ron announced.

There was a moment of stunned silence, followed by staccato applause as the spotlight shifted to light up a delicate blue lace shawl that looked so light it reminded Faith of gossamer.

Francine's expression closed up like a book despite the pasted-on smile she produced.

"Well, I never!" Pearl protested loudly. She turned such a frightening glare on the table of younger Bettys clapping behind them that the group stopped momentarily until Francine stood slowly.

Faith's heart twisted in pity for Francine. Second place in knitting and no placement at all for her beloved bunny. Disappointment radiated from the woman despite her attempt to cover it. This really had been a dreadful week on any number of levels for the club president. Her walk to the podium was slow and painful.

Dinah hugged Francine and whispered something in her ear as she gave her the second-place ribbon.

The moment obviously felt awkward for everyone, and several women murmured condolences and reached out a hand to Francine as she silently trudged back to her seat.

Faith was glad she couldn't hear what Pearl was muttering under her breath on the other side of the table.

"First place goes to Brittany Sawyer's astounding full-length dress," Dinah said. "How she managed to get all that knitting done in such a short time is an impressive feat indeed. It must be all that youthful energy."

"Or it's because she doesn't own a rabbit," Pearl barked. "Honestly, what true Betty doesn't own a rabbit?"

Faith thought of Annette, who didn't own a rabbit but had pulled out her own knitting from the contest to comfort Francine's Beatrice.

"I think we'd all like your amazing speed," Dinah said as the young woman gleefully bounded up to the stage. "I find myself wondering if you even slept."

"I've always been a super-fast knitter," Brittany said. "And Betty audiobooks helped me stay awake to get it done."

"Audiobooks," Pearl sneered. "Whatever happened to chatting with friends while you stitched? Everyone's got things stuffed in their ears while they stare at their phones anymore."

Brittany held up her blue ribbon and grinned.

The younger Bettys cheered.

Whatever anyone thought of Brittany as a Betty, Faith had to admit the long gray dress with the cable design and ruffles at the cuffs really was the most impressive item of the lot.

"I think your shawl is stunning," Faith said to Francine.

The praise seemed to have little effect on Francine's defeated expression. *Defeated* really was the best way to describe it. Francine's sad resignation stood out in stark contrast next to the buzz of boasting Pearl had kept up since her win.

Faith swallowed the urge to tell Pearl to let poor Francine be.

Even the announcement of the rabbit sweater prizes—many of which had been made for Beatrice as well as for the other de-furred rabbits—failed to raise Francine's spirits. In fact, it appeared to Faith that the show of support only made the woman more miserable.

"And now," Dinah said, "let's enjoy each other's company with carrot cake for everyone!"

The rest of the event never quite felt like the celebration it was meant to be. The tension between the older and younger Bettys was thick enough to cut with the knife being used to serve the cake.

Faith rose and made her way toward the dessert table with Wolfe. "Brooke makes the best carrot cake in the world," she whispered to him, "but I doubt it's good enough to smooth over all the ruffled feathers in this room."

"I don't know about ruffled feathers," he replied with a concerned glance around the room, "but the fur is definitely flying here tonight."

12

"That wasn't the pleasant evening I was hoping for," Wolfe said as he and Faith reached her cottage door. He had graciously walked her home after the awards dinner. "The tension in that room was exhausting."

"Just tomorrow and Sunday to go," Faith said. "Dinah looks just about done in. I'm feeling that way myself."

"Well, the evening wasn't a total loss. Dinner was delicious, thanks to Brooke. I really don't know what we would do without her. And I was very grateful for the company. I didn't feel as if I could turn down their invitation, but I wasn't keen to face all that stress on my own."

"You?" Faith teased. "You've got enough charm to be a diplomat. You could have handled that easily without my assistance. But I'm glad you invited me. I did want to see who won those competitions, and I'm glad to have helped. It's been a rough few days for all of us."

"I don't like the idea of murders happening in our library. Anywhere on the grounds, actually, but most especially in the library." He held out his hand for her keys. "Let me try your key. I want to be certain this lock works right." He tried it and had the same difficulty Faith had begun to have last week. "You're sure no bunny's been nibbling on your keys?"

Faith was glad to laugh. "I'm sure."

"After this week, I'd believe you if you said you caught some long-eared fellow chomping on them."

"I think it's only wear and tear. But I'd be lying if I said I'm not at least a little bit spooked by everything that's happened. At least we've still got time to get to the bottom of it. Did you hear Pearl tonight?"

"I did, and I'll tell Garris about the way she was speaking," he said. "But please let the police take care of it. Curiosity is one thing, and you've certainly proven your sleuthing abilities, but if there's any danger, I'd hate for you to get mixed up in it."

"I appreciate your concern, but no one's given me any reason to think I'm in any danger." She pushed open the door—and gasped.

"Watson, on the other hand . . . ," Wolfe quipped as the two of them stared at a massive tangle of yellow yarn strewn about the cottage floor.

The cat in question sat on the couch, obviously unharmed, slowly licking one paw as if he'd been waiting and they were late for curfew.

"Rumpy!" Faith exclaimed as she picked up one end of a seemingly endless tangle of yellow yarn. "What have you done?"

Wolfe bent down to pick up another mass of yellow fiber. "I believe Watson has let his views on cat clothing be known." He held up the bunch of fuzzy yarn. "Maybe there's a reason why only dogs seem to wear sweaters."

Watson jumped down off the couch to brush up against Wolfe's leg in a gesture that looked all too much like agreement.

Faith shook a finger at her cat. "That sweater was a thoughtful gift. No matter what you thought of the idea, all that knitting didn't deserve to meet such a ghastly end." She began picking up the rest of the yellow shreds that covered most of the room. "Maybe Eileen can alter the other two to fit Atticus. After the Bettys leave, though. Those lovely women would be heartbroken to see your commentary on their work."

"At least you were smart enough to pull a stunt like this in the cottage." Wolfe reached down to scratch Watson behind the ears. "If you'd done this anywhere in the manor, you might wake up with no fur at all. It's already happened to a few rabbits there."

"You especially keep away from Pearl, Rumpy," Faith cautioned.

"That woman is the first Betty I've met who sounds mean enough to be the shearer," Wolfe said.

Faith nodded. "Francine is a dear friend of hers, or at least she was. Still, Pearl seems cruel enough to shave those bunnies. And she even admitted that she's glad Maura is gone."

"Not to mention how pleased she was to take first place in the rabbit judging," Wolfe added as he retrieved more yarn. "I felt bad for Francine the way Pearl gloated. Quite frankly, I'd forgotten they were friends until you said so just now."

"A rabbit owner I talked to at the show said the only way anyone would ever take first place was if Beatrice was out of the running. If Pearl wanted it badly enough . . ."

"I'd believe her capable of the shearings, but the murder?" Wolfe asked. "She's got a sharp tongue, but could she have gone as far as that kind of violence?"

Faith put her coat away in the hall closet. "Those rabbit owners would tell you that shearing was an act of violence. And Pearl clearly doesn't like where the Betty Townsend novels are heading."

"She certainly doesn't like the new wave of younger Bettys either," Wolfe said.

"If Pearl saw Maura as the source of both those things, it's possible she killed her. She seems more suspect than any of the other Bettys, if you ask me."

"Well," Wolfe said, yawning, "Garris will get a full report about what we heard from Pearl tonight. He told me he's still investigating everyone. But I think tonight we saw that Pearl has motive."

Faith collected more tangles of yarn. Watson seemed to have spent the entire evening "decorating" the living room of her cottage. "Motive? Absolutely. It's the opportunity piece that has me stumped, though. The library was locked. None of those guests would know Maura was there or have access to the room even if they did. So who could have gotten in there to push Maura over the balcony?"

"Tonight's announcement about the television deal seemed to irritate the older Bettys as much as it excited some of the younger ones. Maybe the news will spur Pearl—or whoever our culprit is—to act again and show themselves." Wolfe found one last strand of what had once been Watson's sweater.

Faith perched on an arm of the couch. "Do you think the murderer and the shearer are the same person? I can't decide if that would make things better or worse." She sighed. "I feel terrible for Dinah. All she wants is for her books to make readers happy, not to launch arguments or incite violence."

"If we can solve both mysteries, there's still a chance for all this to work itself out," Wolfe replied. "On the whole, I'd say the Bettys have been very pleasant guests of the manor. None of Marlene's nightmares about rabbit destruction have come to pass."

Faith walked to the kitchen and pulled a plastic bag out of her cabinet. With a frown, she deposited the unraveled yarn inside. "All that work destroyed in a matter of hours. The whole cats-and-yarn stereotype must really be true."

"At least in Watson's case." Wolfe joined her in the kitchen and added the yarn he'd collected to the bag. "Garris told me your and Midge's theory about those pages. Why would Ron try a stunt like that? And why those particular pages?"

Faith leaned against the kitchen counter, thinking. "I can't be sure, but I believe it has to do with the phone numbers Dinah was upset about."

"What could be so important about fictional phone exchanges that Dinah's notes on them would need to be destroyed? Why put them in bunny cages? There are a dozen other easier and more secure ways to destroy a piece of paper."

"I wish I knew. But there's a book club meeting tomorrow night, and you know my friends have a knack for figuring out things like this. It was Eileen who caught the inconsistency in the first place. Maybe she'll come up with something else when she starts looking." Faith rubbed her temples. "What a mess everything has become."

"Most messes untangle themselves eventually," Wolfe said, buttoning his coat again. "Except for a certain sweater I once knew."

"Really, Watson," Faith said as she walked Wolfe to the door. "I don't know what to do with you."

The cat sat smugly on the back of the couch, yet to show a shred of remorse.

"That's easy," Wolfe said as he gave Faith wink. "Don't put him in any more sweaters."

"Apparently," Faith said. "Good night."

"See you tomorrow, Faith. Sleep well."

As she closed the door and locked it behind Wolfe, Faith wondered if she could.

"I doubt I'll fall asleep quickly anyway, no matter how tired I am," she said, sitting down on the couch.

Watson jumped onto her lap and cozied up to her, purring.

"Nice try, mister, but I'm not ready to forgive you yet."

There were way too many questions buzzing around inside her head. Novels and rabbits and bracelets and fur, then back again.

"This is one of the stranger cases we've ever had at Castleton, isn't it?"

Watson offered no comment.

"You are still not welcome in the library tomorrow," she told him sternly. "You're grounded one more day until the bunnies leave. Things are too tense over there, and I don't want to have to explain why you aren't wearing any of the sweaters those ladies made for you."

The next morning, Faith raised her hand to knock on the door of the Daphne du Maurier Suite, where Dinah was staying. The author had graciously accepted Eileen's request to sign the Candle House Library's stock of Betty Townsend novels, and Faith was picking them up to return to the library when she went to the book club meeting that night.

The door flew open before she could knock, however, and a red-eyed Francine stormed out past her.

"Frannie, don't be this way," Dinah called after her, looking close to tears herself.

Francine marched down the hall without a backward glance.

"I can come back another time," Faith said quickly.

"That's all right. I doubt this will get better anytime soon," Dinah said sadly. "Come in."

Pouf hopped across the floor to her owner as Dinah pulled a tissue from a box on her nightstand and dabbed at her eyes.

"What happened?" Faith asked. "Is Francine still upset over last night?"

Dinah sat on the couch and motioned for Faith to do the same. "I didn't think she'd react quite this badly." The author shook her head. "Then again, who could have predicted what's happened here this week?"

"From what I've seen, Francine has been an admirable leader of the Bettys." Faith took a seat on the couch. "She seems to take her presidency very seriously."

Dinah waved the tissue and sniffed again. "She does, and she's highly respected because of it. Ron and I had asked her to help shore up support for the series' new direction. But I think the shearing was just too much for her. And I knew it would be a blow for her not to take first place in the knitting competition."

"That puts you in a difficult position," Faith commiserated.

"Oh, it does. I told Ron so, even though we both knew Brittany's work was superior. Ron insisted that a younger Betty winning the knitting competition would be a good thing. I couldn't bring myself to fix the results, even for Frannie. The truth is that Lady Latte was the best rabbit and Brittany was the best knitter. So I agreed to the awards as we announced them. Even though I knew it would crush Frannie."

Faith phrased her next question as carefully as possible. "I know this is a difficult question, but do you think there's any chance one of the Bettys' emotions would run high enough over the change in direction to—"

"Harm Maura?" Dinah finished for her with wide eyes. "Absolutely not. My Bettys are as loyal and sweet as they come."

"Some very drastic things have been done in the name of loyalty," Faith said, remembering the sharp tone of Pearl's words.

"No Betty could be a murderer," Dinah protested.

"I'm having trouble believing it could be true as well. But could a Betty be behind the shearings at least?" Faith bit her lip, reluctant to voice her suspicions. But Dinah deserved to know. "Pearl Quinton, perhaps?"

"Pearl? She won."

"Yes, but you could argue that it was because Beatrice was taken out of the competition."

Dinah stood up. "I hate to admit it, but the thought has crossed my mind. But Frannie and Pearl have been friends for years, and I won't believe my Bettys would do that to each other nor to each other's beloved rabbits. That's a line none of them would ever cross."

"Are you sure?" Faith asked gently.

Dinah picked up Pouf and stroked the animal. "I'm positive. They simply wouldn't do anything like that. The culprits must have come from somewhere else." She stared at Faith. "I'll ask you to keep your theories to yourself. Things are bad enough without wild accusations being thrown around."

"I didn't mean to upset you," Faith said honestly. "I'm sorry that this week has gone so terribly. You should be celebrating your tremendous achievements, not struggling to keep peace between factions of your fans."

Dinah's sharp expression softened. She sighed and gave Faith a sorrowful look. "So you see it too—how the older and younger Bettys don't get along."

"It's hard not to," Faith admitted.

"I hate how the split's been widening. The Bettys have always been the best part of my job. They constantly send me cards and letters, little gifts, drawings, all sorts of things."

"That sounds nice."

"Oh, it is." Dinah sat back down, but she kept Pouf on her lap, running her fingers through the soft fur as she spoke. "It's wonderful to know readers love my work. Only—well, fans can be challenging. Enjoyment can sometimes become expectations, and expectations can sometimes become demands."

"I'm not sure I follow you," Faith said.

"They feel Betty is as much theirs as she is mine, and that devotion means they can get quite upset if the books take a turn they don't agree with."

"Like what's happened this year." Faith felt like she had to ask. "Have you been threatened in any way?"

Dinah's hand went to her chest. "Me? Gracious, no. But I do wonder about Ron."

Faith thought of the stairwell argument. "Has he been threatened?"

"He hasn't told me anything, but then again, I'm not sure he would. The Bettys see him as the enemy, you know. They're certain he's making me change the Betty books because it's easier to swallow that idea than the fact that I might want to shift gears a little. I'm sure some of them are convinced I'm being forced to do something I don't want to do."

"But you're not?"

"Ron wants me to play up the drama because it makes the Bettys feel better. I was a bit skeptical of the shift when he and Maura first suggested it, but I really don't mind the changes."

"I guess I'm surprised to hear that, given your success."

Dinah gave a slight smile. "Sixteen books in a tiny Oklahoma town can get tiresome. I might not have chosen a change quite as dramatic as the one those two dreamed up, but then again I never had a television deal until we moved the series to New York and World War I, did I?"

"Why is Ron so upset?" Faith asked.

"I think it's perfectly natural for him to be that upset considering how much he cared for Maura."

"Were Ron and Maura involved?"

"An author must be observant by nature," Dinah replied. "Betty's books have always had a touch of romance, and I'm attuned to the signs."

"I overheard an argument between them the night before Maura was killed. At first I thought it might be a professional disagreement, and of course I told Chief Garris what I'd heard, but . . ."

"Now you're wondering if what you heard was a lovers' quarrel?" Dinah finished for her.

Faith nodded.

"You could be right. Neither of them ever admitted anything of the sort to me, but I could tell that things had been strained between the two of them recently." Dinah's eyes grew sad. "I think they might have made a lovely couple if they could have worked things out."

"Were you rooting for them to be together?" Faith asked.

"I'm not saying it wouldn't have been awkward, or perhaps just complicated, but I'm fond of Ron and want him to be happy."

"Forgive my saying so, but you didn't look very fond of him at lunch the other day because of the manuscript."

Dinah waved the comment away. "We have our rows, Ron and I, but we both know I need him to succeed as much as he needs me to succeed. There'd be no Betty Townsend books without Baxter House, and at the risk of sounding a bit full of myself, Betty's sales have gotten Baxter through a rough time or two. But Ron stooping to hide my words in rabbit hutches? That's going too far."

"You knew it was Ron who did that, and you didn't say anything?"

"What would it solve if I did? It couldn't be undone, and it would only make everything worse." Dinah ran a hand along Pouf's fluffy ears. "The man needs to hire a better proofreader instead of resorting to silly theatrics."

Faith sat back. "So it was Ron who put those specific pages in the rabbit hutches."

"Specific pages? I don't know about that. He probably took a handful off the top and shoved them into their cages while we were having a small argument at the back of one of the seminars on hutch care. The poor man was grieving, so I tried to forgive him."

"It wasn't just a handful of pages," Faith told her. "Every page Dr. Foster recovered from those rabbit cages contained the incorrect phone exchanges."

Dinah blinked at her. "Why would Ron do that? He knows Maura caught the mistakes just like I do. What would be the point of hiding them now?"

This was a new wrinkle. "Maura caught the phone exchange inconsistencies, not you?"

"Maura is—*was* my editor. Catching errors was her job."

Faith thought back to the shouting in the stairwell. "Now that I think about it, I believe that was the argument I overheard. Her calling it off with him because of the phone exchanges."

"Well, that makes no sense. It's a silly thing to have such a fierce argument over." Dinah's hand went to her chest, and her eyes teared up. "Goodness, I just realized. Going over those galleys was the last thing she did for me. God rest her young, ambitious soul. It's all so horribly tragic."

Faith felt as if she'd troubled the poor author enough, so she finished the conversation and collected the signed books quickly.

As she gave Dinah a sympathetic hug and made her exit, one thought kept echoing in her mind. If calling out Ron on those mistakes was the last thing Maura did, was it what had gotten her killed?

With few library tasks to attend to, Faith made her way to the kitchen after her unsettling conversation with Dinah. Today's luncheon and charity book signing were among the final formal events of Betty Townsend Week.

Faith was beginning to worry that the conference would conclude without any solutions to the mystery of the shearing or the larger mystery of Maura's murder. She disliked the thought of all those kind women leaving their favorite event under a dark cloud, and she hoped Brooke could settle her thoughts if not cheer her up.

The chef was busy preparing lunch for the guests, but as she often did, Brooke let Faith enjoy a cup of coffee at the small table that sat at the back of the kitchen on the manor's lowest level. They made conversation as Brooke continued her work.

"I have to say," Brooke said as she sorted through a bowl of strawberries for the luncheon's shortcake dessert, "I'm exhausted. I remember back when I thought this was going to be a ho-hum event."

"With all these bunnies?" Faith was pleased to discover she could still laugh. The company of friends was always good medicine. "I thought it would be interesting, but I don't think I ever want an event to be *this* interesting."

"Oh no, I like the rabbits, and the Bettys are great," Brooke replied. "It's the three M's that have me tired."

"Three M's?" Faith snuck a plump red berry from the bowl and popped it into her mouth.

Brooke ticked them off on her fingers. "Murder, mystery, and Marlene. I'm still wondering if Marlene is going to survive the week." Working in the basement where many of the manor workrooms and offices were located, Brooke often had a front-row seat to Marlene's stresses that the guests on the public floors never saw.

"Still tense, is she?"

Brooke blew a strand of hair off her forehead. "I didn't realize Marlene had this level of tense. All these rabbits and an unsolved murder have taken that woman over the edge. It's made me stressed. Diva and Bling have even picked up on it despite their spiffy new bowl cozy."

"Betty Townsend Week's been hard on everyone, staff and guests alike," Faith agreed.

Brooke pushed aside the bowl of berries and planted a hand on one hip. "Did you know I actually found myself saying a prayer of thanks that the body was found in your library and not in my kitchen?"

"I don't blame you. Being the 'scene of the crime' has made for extra stress, believe me. Usually I consider my library as the bastion of peace at the manor but not this week." Faith sighed. "I'd rather be flooded with research questions than go through another conference like this."

Brooke began pulling ingredients from one of the large stainless steel refrigerators that lined a wall of the kitchen. "How are things with the guests today?"

"Better, I suppose. Still, it's hard to see how anyone will really calm down until we find out who killed Maura and who sheared the rabbits. I don't know that we've gotten any closer to a solution."

"I'm still wondering," Brooke said, gesturing at Faith with a carton of cream. "Are we in search of one culprit or two?"

"Who knows? I was—"

Her remark was cut short by shrieks and frantic footsteps. Marlene burst through the door, terror widening her eyes. "They're eating the library!"

Faith and Brooke looked at each other for a split second before they abandoned the kitchen and sprinted for the stairs behind Marlene. The trio picked up a steady stream of curious Bettys as they raced toward the library.

"Rabbits," Marlene panted. "Confounded free-roaming rodents..."

Books, paper, leather, and heaven knows what else. Faith's thoughts tolled like a warning bell. "I'm absolutely certain I locked the door before I went upstairs to see Dinah," she said as they crossed the Great Hall Gallery, where guests gaped at the staff racing through the halls. "How does it keep getting opened?"

"It's not. The monsters are locked in there with our books," Marlene replied as the three of them skidded to a stop in front of the library door.

True to Marlene's word, Faith found the door locked. When she finally unlocked the door and pushed it open, she wasn't prepared for the sight that met her.

A group of rabbits frolicked happily all over the floor of the room. It was the oddest clash of images: cute, cuddly bunnies gleefully hopping through the formal opulence of the Castleton Manor library.

Gleefully *snacking* on various parts of the library.

Faith, Brooke, Marlene, and the Bettys flooded the room.

"Unthinkable! Kindly remove your beasts from our collections," Marlene snapped at the guests. Faith had never heard her use such a tone with the public before.

Faith leaped out ahead of the crowd to scoop up a brown-and-white bunny as he began chewing on the carpet fringe by her desk.

If it was any consolation, the Bettys seemed equally as mortified by the bunny break-in as Marlene, Faith, and Brooke.

"You ought to be more responsible with your animals!" Marlene shouted as she stood amid the chaos.

"We didn't let our rabbits in here," a woman protested as she pulled a bit of book binding from her rabbit's busy teeth. "We were getting the other room ready for the book signing. Someone kidnapped our bunnies and locked them in your library."

Rabbit-napping? Had the "vandalism shearer" discovered yet another way to strike?

"Goodness, Fletcher, don't eat that!" came a cry from the memoir shelves.

Faith turned in circles, unsure which disaster to address first. No library science class came close to covering what to do in such circumstances. Her brain began cataloging the contents of each low shelf in the library. At the same time, she sent up a prayer of thanks that the manor's rarest books were kept under glass, where curious noses and teeth could not reach. Faith loved pets as much as anyone, but when those pets began gnawing on the collections under her care, that patience came to an end.

"There's one good thing about this. At least that cat of yours wasn't in the library with the rabbits," Marlene grumbled to Faith as she darted around, rattling her massive key ring low to the floor in an attempt to herd the critters.

How true. Watson's presence in the middle of this chaos was the only thing that might have made the whole fiasco even worse than it already was.

Still, Faith didn't have time to borrow trouble. The situation required immediate action. Grabbing a nearby empty box, she swept a pile of papers from one of the research tables. Stepping up on one of the ottomans, she raised her voice over the mayhem. "Everyone! Find your rabbit as quickly as you can. Whatever they were eating or whatever you find that seems to have been nibbled on, please bring it to this table."

Out of the corner of her eye, she spied a small rabbit regarding the straws of the antique broom that was kept on the fireplace hearth. In a swift rescue, Faith plucked the little critter from the hearthstones and held it up. "Whose is this?"

"Oh, that's mine," a woman called. She ran over and took the bunny from Faith. "Rufus, you ought to know better," she scolded.

"How many of them are there?" Brooke called, chasing a rabbit out from underneath a cushioned chair.

"Too many!" Marlene yelled, looking ready to mount one of the ottomans for fear the bunnies would soon turn and start chewing on her.

At the shout, thumping sounds filled the room from all directions. It took a moment for Faith to realize the sounds were coming from the rabbits. "They're stomping?"

"It's how they sound the alarm," one Betty said as she snatched up a small multicolored bunny. "They're frightened, poor things."

As Faith glanced around the room in an attempt to assess the damage, a realization struck her. Each rabbit in the library belonged to the younger generation of Bettys. From what she could tell, none of the older Bettys' rabbits had been let loose as part of this stunt, whatever it was. In fact, none of the older fans were even in the room. Were faction tensions escalating instead of decreasing?

For a nauseating moment, Faith wondered if she'd found herself in the middle of a Betty age war, with her beautiful library as the battlefield.

"What in the world?" Wolfe's deep voice sounded from the doorway amid the calls and yells of women fetching bunnies throughout the stacks. He caught Faith's eye over the commotion. "How?"

"I have no idea," Faith called, trying not to panic. Lots of things had befallen her since taking the job as the manor's private librarian, but nothing had prepared her for a mass rodent attempt to eat the precious collection.

"Gotcha!" another Betty cried. She scooped up her rabbit as it attempted to scurry across the carpet.

The animal kicked and made small grunting noises, and the sound of more stomping filled the room.

"That's it!" Marlene declared, red-faced and furious. "I have tried to be open-minded and patient, but that is it! Take your animals and confine them in cages in your rooms until you leave the premises! No free-roaming rabbits whatsoever!"

For once, Faith found it hard to disagree with Marlene's hard stance. She stared at the pile of nibbled books, bindings, files, and periodicals that were now stacked on the research table. An editor falling to her death from the balcony, vandalism shearings, author-publisher battles, and now bunnies sent to damage her books?

With a sinking heart, she even noticed a few stray gnaw marks on the legs of her chair and desk, not to mention a dozen ragged edges on the rug. Who knew what other literary and furnishing carnage she would find upon further inspection?

It took ten more minutes before the last rabbit was captured and removed from the room. The only stomping to be heard was Marlene's footfalls heading to the library door. She shut it with a declarative *click*. Her frustrated sigh filled the room.

For a long moment, Faith, Brooke, Wolfe, and Marlene stood in stunned silence.

As Faith studied the damage, she tried not to give in to tears. "Where do we even begin?"

"First, we need to send a complete damage report to Baxter House," Marlene said. She grimaced as she glanced around the room. "But with all the destruction they inflicted, I'm not sure an invoice is enough. Would it be possible to ask Mr. Powers to give us a check immediately?"

A heavy pause hung in the air before Wolfe said, "I would demand payment from him right now if I thought it would do any good."

"Any good?" Marlene asked. "That man owes us for all the damage his event has done. I don't care if he paid extra to book us at the last minute. I wouldn't care if he paid triple our usual rate. Nothing is worth the harassment he's caused."

"I agree," Wolfe said. "But getting a check from Baxter House isn't the solution here."

"Whyever not?" Marlene asked with one hand on her forehead. "He's liable. His publishing house should pay for every bit of this."

Wolfe pulled his phone from his pocket. "He should. Baxter House should pay its bills and then some, like any other troublesome guest. But that's exactly why I was coming down to look for you. I just got a call from the bank, and the deposit check from Baxter House has bounced."

14

"Baxter House passed a bad check?" Marlene asked. "After everything they've put us through? Are still putting us through?" She planted her hands on her hips. "The nerve of some people."

"I'm hoping it's all a misunderstanding," Wolfe said, but he didn't sound too confident. "I'm fully prepared to have a firm conversation with Ron about settling his account."

"An account that had better include damages," Marlene replied as she walked back toward the door. "Believe me, you'll have a full accounting of what they owe on your desk within the hour. Faith can assess her own damages and add to it when she's ready." With that, the assistant manager left the room, the sound of her determined footsteps echoing down the gallery.

"What a circus," Brooke remarked. "How about I send up tea to add some calm while you figure out where to start?"

Anything that added calm to this whole crazy situation sounded like a fine idea to Faith. "Thanks, Brooke."

The chef's exit left Faith and Wolfe to stare at the disarray. Piles of damaged books, files, papers, and portfolios filled the table. A pillow and carpet had been nibbled. A drape had a ragged corner. The bunnies had done a startling amount of damage in the short time they were locked in the library.

"Marlene was right," Faith said, feeling her stomach turn to knots as she considered the work ahead of her to restore order. "There's one good thing about this whole mess."

"What could possibly be good about this?" he asked, waving his hand over the pile of damaged materials. He appeared tired and strained, his blue eyes falling far short of their usual sparkle.

"Watson could have been in here. Imagine the chaos then."

"She's right. It would have been absolute hysteria." Wolfe began to laugh. "If Watson had been locked in with all those bunnies, it would have been a madhouse."

"It would, wouldn't it?" Faith was glad to feel laughter bubbling up from the knots in her stomach as she pictured Watson hissing and yowling in an attempt to defend his sacred library from the onslaught of snacking bunnies. "He'd have terrified them. Or they'd have terrified him."

Wolfe put one hand over his eyes and laughed harder. "And I thought the fur flew at last night's dinner." His laughter died down a bit. "I'm sorry about all this. Things have gotten out of hand, and it'll be a lot of work for you to fix it. Please speak up if you need some help putting it to rights."

Faith pulled in a deep breath. "Thanks. I will. At least no one was hurt. Well, no animals or people, anyway. And I don't think any of the really valuable books sustained any harm." She gave him a sideways glance. "Remind me to institute a new policy: all rare and valuable books must be shelved at eye level or higher."

"Done. But what if our next event includes a herd of giraffes?"

"Don't even joke about it," she moaned.

"You're right. I'm sorry. Oh, I meant to tell you. Garris has been looking into the number switches in the books. He's going to question Ron again right after the signing today."

Wolfe and Garris already knew about the business with the phone numbers, and Faith had shared with them how Dinah had confirmed the editor and publisher were romantically involved. "Does he agree that Ron is our murder suspect?"

"Yes, Ron does seem like the most likely option, but he claims to have an alibi. He says he was on a phone call to someone in London at the time of the murder. Garris is checking it out."

"Claiming to be on the phone isn't much of an alibi," Faith countered.

"I admit that it certainly looks bad for Ron, except for one thing."

"What's that?" Faith asked.

"The man seems legitimately heartbroken to me. I had a meeting with Ron after dinner the day we found Maura murdered. The guy was torn apart, to the point where I suggested we reschedule the meeting for when he calmed down. Would he be so grief-stricken if he really was Maura's killer?"

"Love gone wrong has been at the heart of hundreds of murders—real and fictional."

"That's true," Wolfe conceded. "Garris was planning to finish checking Ron's cell phone records before he came up here this afternoon. We'll know soon enough if he was telling the truth."

"Another thing," Faith said. "If it turns out the discovery of those phone numbers was the real motive for murder and Ron alibis out, that would leave Dinah. She's the only other person who knew about them."

"That's true, but I really can't see Dinah hurting anyone," Wolfe said. "Can you?"

"No, not really. She's not that type, and she'd have too much to lose if she's not in favor of Ron editing her work."

"Jilted love aside, I still can't see how something as small as number changes could be a motive for murder."

"The Bettys are scheduled to leave tomorrow. The clock's ticking." She crossed her arms over her chest. "I don't know what it is, but my gut tells me the answer is in those phone exchanges."

"Please make sure you don't sleuth yourself into any danger," Wolfe said seriously.

"That would be easier if I knew who killed Maura and who shaved those rabbits. Oh, and I guess now I can add who sicced a herd of bunnies on the library and whether or not all three incidents are related."

"That's a long list," Wolfe said. "Do you think they're connected?"

"I'm not sure. The only way it makes sense is if the shearings hide evidence of some kind. Like the identity of the rabbit whose hairs were caught in Maura's bracelet. We think hairs that long could only have come from Beatrice or Lady Latte."

"Francine wouldn't take herself out of a competition that was so important to her," Wolfe reasoned.

"Which leaves Pearl. But why? How? If she's the shearer and Ron's the murderer, what do they have to do with each other? I can't fathom it."

"You heard her last night," Wolfe said. "She thinks Baxter House is ruining Betty. She could have easily felt it was Maura's doing."

Faith began counting off suspects on her fingers. "Ron, Pearl, Dinah—any one of them could have pushed Maura off the balcony. That's too many suspects in my book."

"Any murder suspect is too many in my book. Well, I'd best be going and leave you to get started putting things in order. You sure you don't need help?"

"No thanks. I think I'd better tackle it on my own. I can always call Eileen if I need extra librarian hands."

"Who needs my help?" Eileen appeared at the door just as Wolfe was leaving.

They exchanged smiles, and he ducked out.

"I thought I'd drop in early to see . . ." Eileen's words trailed off as she caught sight of the table of damaged materials. "What on earth happened?"

"We've had a bit of chaos this morning. A rabbit invasion," Faith said. Just taking in the destruction around her made her feel tired. She briefly recapped the morning's wild events.

Eileen shuddered. "Makes a librarian's blood run cold." She touched one of the nibbled books in heartbroken sympathy. "Terrible. Who would do something like this?"

Faith sighed. "I don't know. So now we have three crimes to solve at the book club meeting tonight. Murder, bunny assault, and assault bunnies."

Eileen shook her head. "Using bunnies against books. What kind of mind thinks up this stuff?"

"Only the rabbits of the younger Bettys were let loose in here," Faith said, "but I'm too frazzled to even wonder whether that means anything."

Eileen tsked as she surveyed the room. "Thank goodness Watson wasn't here today."

"We all said the same thing," Faith agreed. "I'm starting to think there's no way this public book signing can go off without some kind of disaster."

"So nothing happened at the book signing?" Midge asked as the book club met that night.

"It was the only ordinary event of the whole week," Faith said. "I kept waiting for something drastic to happen, but nothing did."

"What a pleasant surprise," Midge remarked.

Faith sighed. "But we're still no closer to solving our mystery. Chief Garris was going to talk to Dinah and Ron again now that Dinah confirmed Ron and Maura were a couple—or at least had been up until very recently. If he learned something important, I don't know what it is."

"Speaking of drastic, that's really all that's left of Watson's sweater?" Eileen pointed to the bag of tangled yellow yarn.

Midge gave a sympathetic smile. "I won't say I told you so, but..."

Watson made a small grunt and settled deeper into Faith's lap. He closed his eyes indignantly, clearly agreeing with Midge's assessment.

"But you told me so," Faith finished for her friend.

Eileen pulled a strand from the bag, fingering the fiber. "It's beautiful yarn. At least it was before Watson got to it. It's useless now—all snagged and snarled. But let's see those other two sweaters you received."

Faith handed her the other garments the Bettys had knitted.

"Oh, these are lovely," Eileen said as she inspected them. "I agree. They shouldn't go to waste just because Watson can't appreciate them." She leaned down to where Atticus was curled at Midge's feet. "Atticus, come here, boy. One cat's castoff is another dog's pullover."

At the sound of his name, Atticus perked up and trotted over to Eileen.

"You like a nice sweater, don't you?" Eileen picked up the Chihuahua and proceeded to put the first of the two sweaters on the dog.

While Watson pointedly ignored what was going on, Atticus seemed to enjoy the oversize new accessory.

"It is a bit big on the little guy," Eileen admitted. "But that's not hard to fix. I'd only have to move the buttons and take in the sides. It'd take me all of an hour, if that."

Atticus gave himself a shake, then hopped down off Eileen's lap and paraded around the room as if he were on display. The sweater dragged on the floor and draped far over his back end so that his legs were hidden under the knitting. It looked more like the sweater was wearing a Chihuahua head rather than a Chihuahua wearing a sweater. It was a comical sight that made the whole group chuckle.

In response, Watson buried his face in the crook of Faith's arm in an expression that obviously said, "I can't bear to look," which made the whole group laugh even harder.

"If you really can alter them, I certainly won't say no to a pair of new sweaters for him," Midge said. "Especially hand-knitted ones."

"Just don't let Atticus anywhere near the manor in those until the Bettys are long gone," Faith warned. "I wouldn't want them to ever know how little Watson appreciates their handiwork."

"I guess I should be thankful he's never taken a dislike to my tunaroons," Midge said, eyeing Watson's disgruntled posture. "That cat's a tough critic."

"Animals show their emotions in dramatic ways," Brooke said. "Diva and Bling can get very emotional. An owner needs to respect that."

"Watson certainly insists on respect," Faith said. "And heaven knows he gets lots of love. But I think we can all agree to no more sweaters."

"Now that we've solved that problem," Eileen said, "we've got another one to figure out. I've been going through the last three Betty Townsend novels, and I even took advantage of the book signing today to check through different editions of books. Ladies, the issue with the telephone exchanges is bigger than we thought."

"How so?" Faith asked, remembering Dinah's comment.

Eileen passed out sheets of paper with a chart on them. "Up until the last two books, the phone exchanges in the novels are consistent. But in the last two stories, all the phone exchanges are a little bit different. Not only that, but they're slightly altered differently in each book."

"How do you mean?" Brooke asked.

"For example, the bank phone number—the one that's my birthday—stays the same in books one through fifteen," Eileen explained. "But it's one digit off in book sixteen and then two digits off in the latest book. And not just the bank, but every phone exchange in the book is off by a few digits."

Midge glanced up from scanning the paper. "That's too big to be an honest mistake, don't you think?"

"It makes no sense," Faith said. "Why would someone deliberately put a continuity error in Dinah's books? If they wanted to anger her fans or make her look bad, there are plenty of bigger ways to do it than something a reader could just write off as a typo."

"Maybe that's exactly it," Eileen said. "It's a small mistake that most readers wouldn't catch, or they'd think it's a typo. After all, I only caught it because the bank's phone number happened to be my birthday. Otherwise, I doubt that I would have noticed it. Even when I did realize it, a small error like this wouldn't be enough to put me off Dinah's books."

"So there has to be another reason," Brooke said, squinting at the numbers. "I don't see a pattern of any kind. It's not as if they could be phone numbers today. There aren't enough digits."

"Maybe it doesn't have anything to do with why Maura was killed," Eileen suggested. "After all, Ron Powers wouldn't be the first man to take a woman's life because she rejected him."

"That's true," Faith replied, "except that knowing what I know now about Ron and Maura, I'm convinced the argument I overheard was definitely about their relationship and the phone number changes. And they were more than just errors. They were part of the reason she broke it off with him."

"He killed her to keep her quiet," Brooke added.

"Which could mean that something in those digits is worth murdering over," Midge said.

"*If* that's what happened," Faith cautioned.

"Is it too far-fetched to think it might be a code of some kind?" Eileen wondered.

"Maybe, but a code relaying what?" Brooke asked. "To whom? And who made the changes?"

"It could be any number of people at Baxter House," Eileen said.

Faith realized something. "If Maura was murdered for discovering those numbers, it couldn't have been a Betty who did it. The fans wouldn't have that kind of access."

"Which points us back to Ron," Eileen concluded.

"Or Dinah herself," Midge said.

"I still won't believe Dinah Harper is capable of such a horrible thing," Eileen declared.

"I know you love her books," Midge said, "but people can be different in private than they are in public. She's written over a dozen mysteries, several of them with murders. Maybe she's more capable of it than you think."

"No," Eileen said stubbornly. "I just can't see it in her."

"I have to say, the Dinah Harper I've met in one-on-one conversations doesn't seem at all different than how she is with her fans," Faith admitted. "She seems genuinely nice and caring."

"But she might be very good at keeping up a front," Brooke countered.

Midge peered at the paper again. "The answer must be in these numbers. What on earth could they mean?"

"I tried an alphanumeric code," Eileen said. "You know, 1 for A, 2 for B, etc., but the results were gibberish. I even tried working with the corresponding letters on a telephone dial, but I came up with nothing."

"I still think you're onto something. It's got to be a message of some kind," Faith said. "But for whom?"

"Obviously someone who reads the books," Midge responded.

"But that could be anybody. Millions of people buy Dinah's books." Eileen let the paper fall to her lap. "For that matter, anyone who ever checks a Betty Townsend book out of a library has access to whatever these are."

"Still," Faith said, "I don't think they're mistakes. These number changes are deliberate. We just don't know why."

"So maybe that's what Maura knew. Or discovered that Ron knew," Brooke said. "We need to be careful about who we share this information with. It's dangerous." She glanced around the group. "Who knows the numbers were changed besides us?"

"Ron, Dinah, and Maura did, and Wolfe and I heard Ron and Dinah argue about them during lunch," Faith replied. "There may be some Bettys who caught the changes as mistakes, but only we and Dinah know about the timing with Maura and Ron's involvement."

"Ron knew Dinah caught the changes," Midge said. "They were

right there in handwriting on those pages I took from the rabbit hutches and you gave to Garris."

"That must be why he needed to destroy them," Brooke said. "The handwriting on those pages proves that if the changes made it into the printed copies, they were deliberate."

Each woman's expression showed the chilling realization Faith felt skitter down her spine.

"Ron has to be our murderer," Brooke announced.

"I agree," Eileen said. "But I don't think this is enough to arrest him. I have to say, I didn't like him from the start. I don't think he gives Dinah the respect she deserves."

"I've gotten that impression too," Faith said.

"But what about the shearings and the bunnies locked in the library?" Midge asked. "What do they have to do with this?"

"Diversions?" Brooke posed. "A way to get the Bettys more upset and force the event to cancel?"

"Or it could be totally unrelated," Faith mused out loud. "They could be about the rabbit contest. If some of the Bettys are upset about where the books are headed, perhaps it upped the stakes for their recognition as knitters and rabbit owners. Competition got fierce."

"I'll say," Midge said. "Shearing an animal is extreme. But I still maintain that whoever did it knew exactly what they were doing. None of those animals were hurt in any way. Taking that fur was about hurting the owner, not the rabbit. Which means my money's on Pearl Quinton."

"Taking out Beatrice so Lady Latte could grab the top prize," Brooke said.

"But they're friends. Who would do that to a friend?" Eileen reached out to touch Watson. "I'd never do anything so cruel to another animal or to a friend."

Brooke shrugged. "They're an intense bunch, those Bettys. And Pearl isn't exactly a kind person. Maybe she got fed up with taking second place to Francine and Beatrice. Maybe she was hoping she wouldn't get caught so that she and Francine could stay friends. Or maybe she cares less about people than she does about winning."

"It makes the most sense," Midge concluded with a sad exhale. "She'd know how to shear Beatrice and the others without hurting them, and she benefits the most from taking the other rabbits out of the competition. Even if their owners were her friends."

Faith sat up straight. "I think you're right. I believe Ron killed Maura and Pearl is our shearer. But we're still a long way from proving any of it."

15

The cat's human stroked his fur. "Just a little while longer until the Bettys leave."

Being told to stay home did not sit well with the cat. He was not one of those indoor cats who perched on carpeted "kitty condominiums" and stared out apartment windows. He was a free-roaming feline, the kind who came and went at will. He knew ways to get in and out of rooms at the manor in fashions that astounded the humans, and sometimes his person simply failed to see how useful that was.

He'd been trying to point his human in the direction of the important clue. His person—and several of her friends—needed to know about the bag of rabbit fur. He knew where it was, but he had not yet figured out a way to show them. That was why he kept trying to get back into the manor—not to eat any rabbits.

Not that rabbits couldn't be tasty. Or entertaining prey. These rabbits, however, had more hair than the cat would ever find appetizing. He didn't want to eat them—he wanted them to go away. Showing his human where the important clues were would get them to go away more quickly, and that was worth the glares and shrieks he'd endure in the hallway.

"I mean it, Rumpy," his human said, sounding tired. "You have to stay home."

Most humans knew the futility of attempting commands to a cat. Especially this cat. He had important duties to perform and not one but two significant clues to disclose. For not only did he know where the bag of fur was, but he'd uncovered something crucial in the library. If he could not draw his person up to where the bag was, at least he could manage to sneak into the library to show her the new shiny thing he'd found.

They'd never discover it without his help. The cat had to get back to the library tomorrow. His human simply didn't realize how much she needed him. Rabbits eating the library indeed! No cat would ever stoop to such antics. Yarn could be toyed with, shredded maybe, but never, ever books. Books made his person happy.

It was time to take matters into his own paws. He'd go to the library. He'd show her what she needed to see. His human needed his help to break the case, and he'd brave those furry monstrosities to do it.

But that was tomorrow. For tonight, he had to help his person in other ways. Settle on her lap, purr, interrupt all attempts at work until she curled up with him in her favorite fireside chair with a cup of cocoa and a book.

He knew he had succeeded in his mission of mercy when she began scratching his ears and talking to him in low tones. "There were rabbits everywhere in the library, nibbling on books. It's enough to break a library cat's heart." She looked down at him. "I shudder to think what you would have done if you'd been there."

The cat knew what he would have done. He would have drawn upon his supreme predator heritage and driven those beasts out of there with a mighty display of claws and teeth.

"I suppose I should apologize for the sweater," she added.

The cat agreed. But they'd been through enough that he loved her anyway and forgave her readily, especially since she'd given the other sweaters to the dog. He gazed up at her and blinked slowly, a cat's kiss. She could count on him.

"Well," she said, and the cat knew he had changed her mind. "I'll tell you what. If you absolutely behave and promise you will not set one paw outside the library, I'll let you come tomorrow. We can both wave goodbye to the rabbits as they clear out of the manor. And if we're lucky, we can solve our three mysteries as well."

The cat snuggled closer to his human. Mission accomplished.

"A stop at Snickerdoodles always makes a Sunday workday easier," Faith said to Eileen as they turned the corner toward the bakery. "Thanks for meeting me."

"It doesn't take much arm-twisting to get me to come here," Eileen admitted.

"I know. There isn't a single thing here I don't like enough to . . ." Faith's words trailed off as she halted and stepped back, staring through the window.

"What's wrong?" Eileen asked.

Faith covertly pointed to a young woman seated in animated conversation with an older woman at the table by the window. "That's Annette."

Eileen raised a questioning eyebrow. "Who?"

"One of the Bettys. Garris told the guests not to leave the manor grounds. Why would she disregard his request like that?"

"I like a good cupcake as much as the next person, but that wouldn't make me—oh!" Eileen's voice pitched up in surprise. "Well, that might explain something."

"What?" Faith tried to get a closer look through the window without drawing attention.

"Wait a minute," Eileen murmured, fiddling with her smartphone. "I'm searching for a picture to be sure."

Faith watched the older woman reach out and touch Annette's shoulder. What was going on?

"I'm right," Eileen said after a moment. "I was sure I recognized her."

"You met Annette," Faith whispered. "She was at the rabbit show."

"Not her, the other woman." Eileen held up a photograph from some book event two years earlier in New York City. It was the same woman sitting with Annette. "That's Claudia Ferguson."

Faith peered at the photograph, then through the window, and finally stared at her aunt. "You're right. Didn't Pearl say Claudia declined the invitation to come this year?"

"If she did, then what's she doing in Lighthouse Bay?"

"And talking to Annette Higgins?" Faith added.

"Should we go in and ask?"

"I don't think so," Faith said. "We may not want to tip them off. Claudia obviously doesn't want people to know she's here. We'd better figure out why before we do any confronting."

Eileen gave Faith a long look. "You don't think . . . ?"

Faith had come to the same unsettling conclusion. "Who'd have more motive to get rid of Maura Webber than Claudia Ferguson? She'd need a guest to let her into the manor before dawn. Maybe Annette is her accomplice." Faith couldn't imagine how sweet Annette would do such a thing, but they owed it to Maura to chase down every lead.

"We can't let her get away," Eileen said.

"If we let her know we're suspicious, we'll scare her off. But if she thinks she's undiscovered, she'll probably stay to the end of the event. Today's supposed to be the final day anyway. I'll talk to Annette when she returns to the manor and see what I can learn." Faith pulled Eileen back toward the far corner of the street. "I'll just have to get my muffin from the manor coffee shop this morning."

Eileen nodded. "Keep me posted. This mystery gets more complicated every minute."

Faith dialed the kitchen the moment she arrived at the manor.

"How's it going? Any word from Garris?" Brooke asked without preamble.

"No. Something else." Faith quickly filled Brooke in on the

appearance of Dinah's former editor talking to Annette Higgins in Snickerdoodles.

"Sounds suspicious all right. Give me a minute to get the quiches in the oven and I'll come up."

A few minutes later, Brooke appeared in the library with coffee and muffins. "Since you had to forgo your Snickerdoodles treats, I stopped in to see Iris on my way here," she explained as she handed a mug to Faith.

"You're the best," Faith said. "Thank you."

"Wow." Brooke scanned the stacks on the research table, now sorted into piles by degree of damage. "Those bunnies can be destructive. It makes me glad I own fish."

"I suppose with how we welcome animals here at Castleton, it was bound to happen at some point." Faith motioned to a nibbled portfolio. "But I never dreamed it would be on this level."

"So why do you think Dinah's former editor is hiding out in Lighthouse Bay and not here at the event?"

"The obvious answer is pretty disturbing. Eileen and I think Annette let her in to kill Maura."

Brooke sipped her coffee contemplatively. "It's possible, but she'd have to know Maura was in the library, and you said only you and Marlene knew where she was."

"I hadn't thought of that," Faith said. "It doesn't all add up easily, does it?"

"No, but it does look bad. What do we do? Tell Garris? Dinah?"

"First, I'll talk to Annette and see if she'll admit to being off the grounds and talking to Claudia. If that really was Claudia. Eileen only knows her from a photograph, so there's a small chance it's not her."

"Pretty small chance. You and I both know there's something going on." Brooke glanced around the library to make sure they were alone and added in a low voice, "Even if she isn't the murderer, could

Claudia have sheared the champions and let the rabbits loose in here? Could she be trying to undermine the whole event as payback for being let go?"

"That's possible too," Faith agreed. "If she's still in town, then that means she's not finished yet."

"Neither is Marlene," Brooke said. "When I walked past her office just now, she was typing fast and furious on her keyboard, which can only mean she's writing a whole host of new rules and regulations. She's talking about permanently banning animals from the library and a whole bunch of other rooms."

Faith frowned. "That's not a solution. Claudia or whoever did this wouldn't have paid attention to rules and regulations anyway. Besides, it would limit guests' ability to enjoy the library, and I don't want that either. Most of all," Faith said, motioning to Watson where he had been sitting in front of some bookshelves for the past hour, "I'd have to ban my valuable assistant over there."

"Well, we can't have that," Brooke said. "Watson's practically a member of the staff."

"I can't run this place without him."

Watson gave them a smug look.

"What do you suppose has got him so interested over there?" Brooke asked, peering at the shelf where Watson sat.

"You know, he's been staring at that spot since we got here. What's up, Watson?"

At the mention of his name, Watson began batting furiously at the far corner of a shelf, stretching his paw underneath and twitching his stump of a tail.

"Is there something under there, Rumpy?" Faith bent down, but she could only see that whatever held Watson's interest was far back under the shelving. "Brooke," she called over her shoulder, "could you bring me the flashlight from the top drawer of my desk?"

"Sure." Brooke retrieved the flashlight and handed it to her.

Faith switched it on to shine into the far corner under the shelf. A small black rectangle was visible among the dust. "Will you look at that? Well done, Watson. Brooke, grab that poker from beside the fireplace and bring it over here so I can slide whatever this is out from underneath the shelf."

Brooke brought over the poker. "What is it?"

Faith slid the long, slender tool under the shelf until a black device popped into view. "A cell phone! Garris told Wolfe they hadn't found Maura's in her room, but a GPS ping showed that it was somewhere on the manor grounds." She picked up the phone and held it up. "Do you think this is it? Ron said he called it a dozen times."

"If she was doing yoga, she probably silenced it." Brooke took the phone from Faith and examined it. "It's the same brand as mine. The battery must be dead by now, so let me run downstairs and get my charger." She hurried out of the library.

A few minutes later, Brooke returned with her charger and plugged it in.

Faith and Brooke waited anxiously.

When it was sufficiently charged, Brooke pushed the button on the top of the phone, and the screen lit up. Then she handed it to Faith.

She swiped the screen to see notifications for a host of missed calls from Ron Powers. "This must be Maura's phone." She glanced at Brooke. "Who doesn't keep their phone password protected these days?"

Brooke shrugged. "People younger than us. They don't care about privacy or security." She pointed to an icon on the screen. "Tap that to view the texts. It'll tell you if it's Maura's for sure."

Faith tapped it, and a new screen filled with long strings of texts from several people including Ron and Dinah. "It is hers. Check this out." She tilted the phone so Brooke could see Ron's texts and Maura's replies. "They were definitely involved."

Brooke took the phone from Faith and began scrolling back through the conversation. "The earlier ones are all affectionate, but these latest are obviously a breakup argument. Oh, but wait, now she gets into it with him." She pointed to a text in all capital letters.

I KNOW WHAT YOU'RE UP TO, AND I'M GOING TO THE POLICE.

"You can't get more suspicious than that," Brooke said. "Maura was onto Ron, and he killed her for it."

"Garris needs to see this right away," Faith said. "This is the evidence we've been searching for."

Brooke nodded, still scrolling through the messages. "They were really serious. He was making big plans for them. There's talk in here of trips, presents, and a lot about their future together."

"How did he go from that to pushing her off a balcony unless he was hiding something?" Faith said. "And remember, the publishing house's check to us just bounced. Something very fishy is going on."

"I'll say." Brooke glanced up from the phone. "What do you think Ron had done that Maura was going to report to the police?"

"I don't know, but I'd bet it had to do with the phone number changes. Maura must have figured out what Ron was doing with those alterations to Dinah's manuscript." Faith dashed to her desk. "I'm calling Garris. He needs to get over here right now."

"There's no need," Wolfe said from the doorway. Dinah was right behind him. "Garris is already on his way."

"Why?" Brooke asked.

Dinah held up a set of oversize scissors, her eyes filling with tears. "Because we found these."

"Rabbit shears?" Faith said, feeling like today had suddenly become even more complicated.

"That's right," Dinah said. "Your veterinarian said she thought those darlings were hand-clipped, not gone over with an electric clipper. This was the weapon used in the attacks—I'm certain of it."

"Where did you find them?" Brooke asked.

Dinah sighed. "In Annette Higgins's knitting bag."

16

"Annette?" Faith's stomach iced over at Dinah's discovery. Suddenly it was hard to think of Annette as the friendly young woman who had knitted a sweater for Francine's Beatrice.

"Annette, if you remember, doesn't own a rabbit," Dinah declared. "Why else would she need the shears if she didn't have a rabbit to use them on?"

"It is suspicious," Wolfe agreed.

Wait until you hear what we know, Faith thought.

"Midge also said whoever sheared those rabbits knew what they were doing," Brooke added. "Wouldn't that mean it isn't Annette?"

"We don't know anything about her other than she's been very good at getting friendly with lots of the other Bettys," Dinah answered. "Pearl tells me she's missed several of the events and meals. As a matter of fact, no one seems to be able to find her right now. I started asking if anyone had seen her because she left her knitting bag in the salon."

"I know where Annette is," Faith piped up. "Or at least where she was earlier this morning. I saw her in Snickerdoodles."

"Why was she in town?" Wolfe asked. "No one is supposed to leave the grounds."

"She was meeting with someone," Faith answered. "Eileen recognized the woman as Claudia Ferguson."

"Claudia is here?" Dinah sounded shocked.

"Probably not on the estate but at least in Lighthouse Bay."

"That can't be. I just spoke to Claudia on the phone last night." Dinah sat down on one of the library's chairs. "Well, that explains how quickly she said she could get here. Cut short her travels to meet me, hmm? I thought it was dedication, but it sounds much more like deception."

"Why did you call Claudia?" Faith asked.

"I made a decision last night to bring Claudia back on board. I need a team I can trust around me right now, and Claudia's as good as they come." Dinah narrowed her eyes. "Or so I thought. Now I'm not sure what to think."

"I can't blame you for wanting a team you can trust," Wolfe said. "But is it your decision? Your editor is an employee of Baxter House."

Dinah straightened with a fierce expression. "That may be true, but Betty Townsend brings in a lot of profits for the publishing house. If my editor wasn't my decision, I'll make it mine now. Perhaps I've let too many other people influence my thinking where my own career is concerned. And my next decision is to locate Annette Higgins and Claudia Ferguson and find out what's going on."

"You may want to wait until you hear what we've found," Faith advised, taking a seat next to Dinah.

The author slumped her shoulders. "What now?"

"We just found Maura's cell phone. I'm afraid the messages on it implicate Ron." Faith showed Dinah the threat from Maura to go to the police with whatever she'd discovered about him. "I think he killed her."

Dinah's eyes widened in alarm. "Ron killed Maura?"

"It certainly seems that way," Brooke said. "He had to silence her when she realized he'd been altering the phone exchanges in your books."

"Why would Ron make those changes?" Dinah asked. "What could he want with those mistakes?"

"We don't know what they are, but we don't think they're mistakes," Faith said.

"Ron killing Maura and putting mistakes in my books. Claudia in town but not at the event. I can't fathom any of it." Dinah seemed to sway in her seat. "How many people are trying to hurt me? And who killed Maura?"

"There's only one way to find out," Wolfe put in grimly. "Confront Ron with the texts and confront Annette with the shears."

Dinah sighed. "I'm supposed to be presenting a check to the Rabbit Rescue League today, not deciding which criminal to accuse first."

Wolfe placed a comforting hand on her shoulder. "I know this is difficult for you. We'll stay with you while Chief Garris walks us through what to do next. I'm sure there are procedures that need to be followed. But I'm certain he'll question Ron and get to the bottom of it. We'll help you find Annette and Claudia."

"Would you like us to call Francine?" Faith asked, feeling sorry for the barrage of betrayal Dinah was suffering. "Or another of the Bettys you're close to?"

"Heavens, no." Dinah waved her hand, dismissing the idea. "Francine has been through enough already. I'm not going to burden any of them with this until we know what the facts are."

"That's understandable," Wolfe said.

"But you can bet I'll make sure Francine knows when we're certain who sheared her Beatrice. Cruelty to animals is a crime, and I want the perpetrator punished." Dinah closed her eyes, collecting herself for a minute. "I want justice done for Maura, for the Bettys, and for their rabbits. I'm prepared to see this through until that happens."

"You're as brave as your heroine," Faith said. "I have no doubt you and the Bettys will come through this ordeal stronger than ever."

Faith watched Ron pace the salon. They'd decided to divide and conquer, with Faith and Wolfe sticking to Ron while Dinah and Brooke went off to see if Annette had returned. They'd told Ron he had to stay in this room with them under the pretense of waiting on word from the bank about the bad check. In actuality, they were waiting on Chief Garris.

Garris was late, although Faith couldn't imagine what might delay a police chief from questioning a prime murder suspect. Garris now knew they had Maura's cell phone, and Faith had given him a summary of the texts between Ron and Maura.

Ron knew none of this, but he must have suspected something because he was showing far more anxiety than a bounced check ought to produce.

The publisher pulled at the collar of his shirt. "Look, Mr. Jaxon, it's awkward I know, but you're a businessman. You understand cash flow can be a tricky business."

Wolfe didn't reply, nor did he meet Ron's eyes.

Faith avoided Ron's gaze as well. Tension filled the air and made the back of Faith's neck prickle. They were in the room with the man who murdered Maura. What was taking Garris so long?

Ron seemed to take Wolfe's silence as doubt. "We've been investing in a good deal of promotion for Dinah's new book in advance of the television series," he continued. "We've had to do a lot of schmoozing, including trips to the coast, that sort of thing."

Again, Wolfe offered no reply.

Wolfe's silence only seemed to increase Ron's panic. "Sales are going to be spectacular," Ron went on, his voice pitching higher and his footsteps getting faster. "Of course, it takes a while for that to translate into cash in the bank. But I've said I'll make good on the check, and I will."

Finally, there was a knock on the salon door, and Chief Garris entered the room. "Sorry for the delay, but I think you'll soon understand why."

Ron looked startled at the police chief's arrival. "You arrest people for one bounced check? Isn't that a bit extreme?"

Faith found it telling that Ron used the word *arrest*. Why assume

Garris was going to arrest him unless he was truly guilty of more than bouncing checks?

"We called Chief Garris," Faith said as she pulled Maura's cell phone from her pocket, "because we found this."

"Maura's phone!" Ron exclaimed. "Where on earth did you find it?"

"It slid under the back of one of the library bookshelves," Faith answered. "Probably when she . . . fell."

"Probably when she was pushed," Garris corrected with a serious look.

"You already told us you know she was pushed," Ron said. "What's going on?"

"We know about you and Maura," Faith said. "We've read the texts."

For a moment, the man's face registered surprise. Then he lunged for the phone. "Those are private."

Faith evaded him and handed the device to Chief Garris instead. "I heard you and Maura arguing in the stairwell the night before she died. I didn't know what it was about then, but I have a good guess now."

"What are you talking about?" Ron asked.

"I don't think you're in any position to be cagey, Mr. Powers," Chief Garris said. "Especially not after what I've learned today."

"What do you mean, what you've learned? I loved Maura. We were going to get married. If you read those texts, then you know. I was setting us up for a future together. She just panicked—that's all. She didn't understand."

"She understood enough to threaten to go to the police. That's why you killed her," Garris said as he slipped the phone into an evidence bag with deliberate slowness.

"No!" Ron cried. "I didn't kill her. I couldn't kill her." Here was a glimpse of the heartbroken man Wolfe had described.

Could it really be possible that Claudia had somehow conspired with Annette to kill Maura? Faith's brain reeled with the possibilities.

The chief placed the phone down on the table beside him. "A few days ago, I began a routine inquiry into the finances of Ms. Harper, Miss Webber, and Baxter House. It doesn't always show up at first, but nine times out of ten there's a money trail to follow in cases like this."

Ron sank into a nearby chair, his face paling. His whole body seemed to deflate with the evidence he saw now building around him. His future was dissolving before his eyes.

"This one was no exception," Garris went on. "Then Wolfe informed me that your company's check had bounced. And Faith shared Miss Webber's text about threatening to go to the police. It didn't take long to figure out what Miss Webber knew. What you killed her to protect."

"I didn't kill her," Ron repeated, his voice sounding more desperate.

Garris continued as if he hadn't heard. "When I was interviewing guests, one of them went on and on about how Ms. Harper has hit the best-seller lists with her last three books. Big sales numbers. Nothing to make anyone think you'd be passing bad checks."

"I was just telling Jaxon here how hitting the lists doesn't always translate into ready cash," Ron said. He wiped his forehead with the back of his hand. "I passed a bad check. I didn't kill Maura."

"Which left me wondering what it was Miss Webber threatened to take to the police," the chief said. "Fortunately for us, it didn't take too much digging with my friends in New York to find out."

Ron stilled and fell silent.

Garris pulled a notepad from his pocket and thumbed through it to a specific page. "Killing Miss Webber only bought you a little time, Mr. Powers. You were already under investigation for embezzlement."

Wolfe's face registered the same shock that chilled Faith.

"Skimming off the profits of his own publishing house," the chief said. "For over a year, they've seen evidence of supposed promotional money being siphoned into offshore bank accounts through a maze of third parties. The only thing they can't work out is how the account numbers are being communicated to his conspirators."

"The phone exchanges!" Wolfe and Faith said simultaneously.

"Chief Garris, I told you Ron's been altering telephone numbers in Dinah's novels." Faith turned to Ron. "Maura discovered what you were doing in those supposed mistakes, didn't she? The texts, the argument I overheard—you weren't just arguing about your future. She'd broken it off with you and was going to turn you in."

"She was never supposed to know," Ron blurted. "I didn't want her involved. I didn't want any guilt on her if it ever came to light. But she was too persistent."

"You were using the alterations to communicate bank account numbers," Faith continued. "That's why the first number to get switched was the bank in Betty's town."

"You killed her before she exposed you," Garris pressed.

"No!" Ron cried out. "I didn't kill her. I told you I was on the phone with a hotel in London arranging accommodations for Dinah's press tour that morning. I was going to propose to Maura while we were over there." He buried his face in his hands. "I was putting together our future at the same time someone was killing her."

His genuine anguish began to make Faith wonder. All the evidence pointed to him, and he clearly had motive. But then again, Claudia also had motive.

Wolfe, Garris, and Faith traded glances while Ron sank into a chair.

"The thing is," the chief went on, "the London hotel confirms they spoke with you at the time you claim."

"See?" Ron replied. "I told you."

"They confirm they took a call from a man using your cell phone," Garris clarified. "That doesn't verify it was you doing the talking. For all I know you could have had someone else placing that call from your phone while you were ending Miss Webber's life."

"No," Ron howled. "It wasn't me. I didn't kill Maura."

"If you didn't kill Miss Webber, then who did?" the chief asked with growing irritation.

Faith took a deep breath and said, "Claudia Ferguson."

"What's Claudia got to do with anything?" Ron asked. "She's not even around."

"She is," Wolfe said. "Faith and her aunt saw Annette Higgins talking to a woman they believe is Claudia Ferguson in a bakery in town this morning."

"She left the grounds after she was warned not to?" Garris asked in dark tones.

"Now do you believe I didn't kill her?" Ron moaned. "Why won't anyone believe me?"

"Motive, opportunity, what's on that cell phone—"

"Anyone could have been in the library at that hour," Ron protested.

"No, that's not true," Faith said. "We don't leave the library open while it's unattended. Certainly not at that hour. I don't know how anyone got in there, whether it was you or Claudia or someone else."

"I'll get to Ms. Ferguson next," Garris said, then turned to Ron. "But you're my primary suspect in this murder investigation. All your denials won't change that. You are not to leave the premises unless you leave in the hands of the federal authorities who will be here in a matter of hours." After a dramatic pause, he added, "Remember this—the question is not whether you'll be arrested. It's just for how many crimes."

"I loved her. I didn't kill her," Ron repeated in a voice that wrenched Faith's heart.

Whether or not he really was the murderer, it was clear that Ron had loved Maura. Perhaps he still did. But had the rejection of that love driven him to murder?

Or had someone else—someone like Claudia—pushed Maura off the balcony?

"Officer Tobin is waiting outside to escort you to your guest room, where you will remain until further notice," Garris told Ron. "He'll be posted outside your door to make sure of it. I'd suggest a call to your attorney, but you are to have no other contact with staff or guests and certainly not with Ms. Harper."

Dinah. Faith's heart went out to the woman. It seemed as if she was losing every ally at a crucial point in her career.

What was happening upstairs right now in Annette's room? Suddenly nibbled bindings seemed like a tiny problem in comparison.

17

Word of the shears being found in Annette's bag had spread among the Bettys with alarming speed. Garris had gone off to find and interrogate Claudia, and Dinah had secluded herself in her suite, so Faith decided it was time to knock on Annette's door.

"They think I did it," the young woman said, not even bothering with a hello. "They think I sheared those rabbits. They think Mom did worse." Tears welled in her eyes. "They think my mom killed Maura Webber."

Faith had to grab the doorway for support. "Claudia Ferguson is your mother?"

Annette stepped aside to let Faith enter the room. "I'm not here just as a Betty. I mean, I am a Betty—I've been a fan since I could read—but I'm here for Mom." She sank onto the end of the bed. "My name isn't really Annette Higgins. It's Anne Ferguson."

Faith took a seat on the chair opposite the bed. "What's going on?"

Anne adjusted her glasses. She suddenly looked very young. "Dinah hasn't seen me in years and I thought she wouldn't recognize me, so Mom offered to pay my way to come to the event and . . . well . . ."

"Spy?" Faith finished for her.

Anne straightened up, her voice gaining an edge. "They never should have let Mom go the way they did, cast off like old clothes or something. Betty Townsend was Mom's life. She built her career on those books. She and Dinah were a team, and Dinah let Ron talk her into changing everything."

Rather than reply, Faith chose silence. The more Anne talked, the more Faith would learn about what was really going on.

"It was Ron's idea to bring Maura on as her new editor," Anne continued. "Maura made all those changes. Nobody likes them, you know. I told you I liked the new direction of the books, but I don't. And Mom hates them."

Faith asked carefully, "Did you shear those rabbits?" While difficult, this question seemed far easier than asking Anne if she was an accomplice to murder.

Anne's eyes hardened. "I didn't do anything like that. I'd never do something so cruel."

"So how did the shears end up in your knitting bag when you left it in the salon?"

"I don't know. I certainly didn't put them in there. I didn't even know what those things were until Dinah accused me."

For a moment, there was enough venom in her tone to make Faith wonder if she really had sheared those rabbits. Avenging her mother was a powerful motive, but then why shear Francine's rabbit and the others? Wouldn't it be Dinah—and therefore Pouf—she'd want to humiliate?

"So you were only here to find out what's going on without your mother as Dinah's editor?" Faith asked.

Anne nodded.

"Dinah had called your mother back into service. Is that what she was telling you in the bakery this morning?"

"She was really happy about it," Anne said. "Glad to get back with Dinah, you know?"

"Are you sure that will still happen now that Dinah knows what your mother and you were really doing?" Faith asked. "Do you realize your mother is now a suspect in Maura's murder?"

"She can't be!" Anne shouted.

"She is. And Chief Garris will likely believe she would have needed your help to do it," Faith said. "If you've made some mistakes here, it will go much better for you if you admit them now."

"Get out!" Anne yelled. "Get out of here right now!"

"Please, I'm just trying to help."

"No you're not. No one is. Just go away!" Anne broke down and sobbed.

As Faith closed the door behind her, one thought pounded through her mind: if they didn't uncover who really killed Maura and who sheared those rabbits soon, there might be nothing left of Dinah's career to save.

"What I simply will not do," Dinah said as she paced her room, "is consider the possibility that Claudia's daughter somehow snuck her into this building at dawn to do away with Maura. It's absurd."

"Lots of things about this case are absurd," Chief Garris pointed out. "If there was ever a case of truth being stranger than fiction—"

"Please don't say that," Dinah begged.

Garris cleared his throat. "Let's review what we know, shall we?" He opened his notepad. "The coroner's office has established Maura Webber's time of death to be between five and five thirty on Tuesday morning. She was pushed off the balcony of the library by an unknown assailant. We now know she was in a relationship with your publisher, Ron Powers."

Dinah nodded. "I suspected they were involved, and things seemed strained between them lately."

"We know Miss Webber had discovered the changes to the numbers in the manuscript," the chief went on. "And we know she knew enough of Ron's crimes to go to the police."

"Maura must have known or suspected the embezzlement," Faith said. "Finding Ron's changes in themselves wouldn't be reason for murder."

"But love would," Garris answered. "Love, money, and murder have gone hand in hand for a long time."

It was possible, but Faith's gut was starting to tell her that while Ron had done many questionable things, it was possible he hadn't murdered Maura. Did that mean Claudia had?

The chief flipped a page in his notepad. "We don't know if the rabbit hairs found in Miss Webber's bracelet could identify her killer. But according to Midge, it's very likely they came from one of two possible rabbits, based on color and length."

The rabbit hairs. That clue didn't point to either Ron or Claudia, so what did it mean?

"I don't think the shearings are related to the murder," Faith said. "I think Pearl just wanted the chance to win the competition. By planting the shears on Anne, she not only deflected guilt, but made the younger Bettys look bad at the same time. She doesn't like the books' new direction, nor does she think the younger fans deserve to be here. Pearl is the one person who would benefit most from Beatrice being shorn. She might even be the one who put the rabbits in the library."

Dinah dropped into a chair. "She and Francine are close friends, not to mention the owners of the other two rabbits that were shorn. Bettys just wouldn't do that to each other. I won't believe it. I won't believe every single person I trusted has turned on each other and against me."

Garris straightened. "I think it's time I talked to Mr. Powers again. And Ms. Ferguson and her daughter." He gave Dinah a determined glance. "Our murderer is here at the manor, and we will find him or her."

Faith was taking a breath to express her hope of the same result when a commotion rose out in the hall.

The shouting brought everyone to their feet. Garris was the first one out the door.

"Get him away!" Francine shouted. "Get that horrid beast away from me!"

As Faith and Dinah followed Garris into the hallway, Faith heard a scuffle and a yowl that could only be Watson. She dashed out ahead of Garris to see Francine standing in her doorway, Pearl behind her, squared off against a hunched and hissing Watson.

"Watson!" Faith exclaimed, dashing toward her cat.

Anne was out of her room, looking as alarmed as Faith. "She tried to kick your cat," she said to Faith while pointing at Francine.

Francine responded by jabbing a finger at Watson. "He's been stalking Beatrice. That beast has been prowling around my door for an hour. He wants to eat my rabbit, I tell you."

Faith went to pick up Watson, but he evaded her grasp and darted away down the hall. *I'll have a word with you later*, Faith thought. "I'm so sorry, Francine. I can't believe Watson meant you or Beatrice any harm."

The chief raised his arms to the gathering group. "Let's all try to calm down."

But Francine ignored him. "Hasn't my poor girl suffered enough?" she demanded. "Haven't I suffered enough?"

Pearl came out from behind Francine, glaring at Anne. "Yes, young lady. Haven't you harmed Francine and Beatrice enough? I hope you're ashamed of your—"

"I'll thank you to stop talking to my daughter that way." Claudia emerged from the room behind Anne.

"Claudia?" Francine gasped. "You're here?"

"I've only just arrived," Claudia replied.

At the manor, Faith added silently, *but not to town*.

"Hello, Claudia." Dinah spoke for the first time, her tone cool and sharp. Her gaze traveled to Anne. "Ah, now I see the resemblance. You've changed a great deal in the last few years, but I should have recognized you."

"You're Claudia's daughter?" Pearl exclaimed.

Faith took careful note of each woman's reaction to the news. After all, if one of them had indeed framed Anne for the shearing, they would likely regret it when they learned they'd framed the daughter of the beloved editor.

Heaven help us get to the bottom of this, Faith thought. *Untangle* really was the perfect word for what would have to happen to solve these mysteries.

"Does this mean you're coming back?" Francine asked, astonished.

"Dinah had asked me," Claudia replied.

Faith found her use of the past tense rather telling.

"Finally, Dinah's come to her senses," Francine said. "Everything was going to absolute ruin without you."

This new sentiment from Francine shocked Faith and evidently everyone else in the hallway. Despite Francine's bolstering the group and supporting Dinah's new direction with the books, it seemed that she actually felt very differently.

The tension in the hallway rose further still as Ron's door opened and he peered beyond Officer Tobin with surprise. "What's going on out here?" His eyes went wide as he recognized his former employee. "Claudia?"

"I called her last night to come back to work for me," Dinah said in a defiant tone that lacked any of the author's usual graciousness. This was the first time they'd seen each other since Ron's financial crimes had come to light. "After all, I need someone to edit my work now that Maura is dead and you're going to jail for embezzlement. If not more."

"Embezzlement?" Francine gaped, glancing from Ron to Dinah. "He stole from you?"

"No, he stole from his own publishing house," Dinah said. She turned to Claudia. "While other people lied to me and sent spies."

The looks exchanged among all the assembled guests in the hallway could have frozen Lighthouse Bay.

Faith could see that the team that had built Betty Townsend might very well be destroyed forever.

Ron broke the silence. "Which one of you killed my Maura?" he yelled. He threw himself forward, but Officer Tobin caught him.

"Your Maura?" Claudia snapped. "Is that how she stole my job? By being *your* Maura?"

"Maura stole no one's job," Dinah said sternly. "And she certainly didn't deserve to die."

"Well, someone here doesn't feel that way," Anne said, mirroring her mother's defensive stance. "Someone is evil enough to murder. Maybe it's the same person who framed me for harming defenseless rabbits."

"You're such a fake," Pearl accused. "Only someone who doesn't own a rabbit herself could do such terrible harm to someone else's."

The raised voices served to attract more guests, as many of the hallway doors opened and more people peeked out to see what was going on.

"You are all awful!" Anne cried. "Betty would be ashamed of every one of you."

"Stop it! Just stop it! The bunnies weren't harmed!" Francine blurted out. "They were sheared, but they weren't hurt. Why can't anyone understand that?"

The hallway fell silent at Francine's outburst.

"*Whoever* did it didn't harm the bunnies," Francine corrected with a frantic emphasis as she backed into her room.

Faith stared at Francine as the facts came together in her brain. She suddenly realized why Watson had parked himself outside Francine's room. Why Beatrice's long white hairs needed to be cut. Why she'd been so reluctant to accept help for Beatrice. "You sheared Beatrice yourself, didn't you?"

For a stunned moment, no one said a word.

It was Pearl who spoke first, her face white with shock. "Frannie? Gracious, you'd never . . ."

Francine's face contorted as she wheeled on her friend. "Never what? Be mean like you, say what I really think? Sit there and swallow what they're doing to Betty? Speak out against that ridiculous impostor of an editor who couldn't diagram a sentence with a gun to her head?"

Pearl's hand went to her chest. "You sheared your own sweet Beatrice? Why?"

"I had to," Francine whimpered. "There wasn't any other way."

Dinah slumped against the wall. Chief Garris and Faith exchanged wary glances. Claudia and Anne clutched each other.

There was only one reason why the fan club president would do such a terrible thing to her own precious rabbit. The realization sent a chill down Faith's back that had nothing to do with the February winds outside.

Anne was the first one to recover the power of speech. "You hurt your own rabbit—and other people's too—and blamed me."

Claudia grabbed her daughter's arm and pulled her back.

"Frannie," Dinah said with an eerie softness as she straightened up from against the wall, "what are you saying?"

Francine waved her arms, her eyes wild. "'Be nice, Francine.' 'Let someone else win for a change, Francine.' 'It's a new world, Francine.' 'You're no longer needed, Francine.' Imagine. Me, no longer needed. I built this fan club."

Faith had the chilling sensation that she was seeing the real Francine for the first time. Everything else had been a mask.

"Maura told me to step down," Francine continued as she glared at Dinah. "Did you know that? She looked me straight in the eye and told me to announce I was resigning my post as president of the Bettys. She didn't ask. She told me. She knew you'd never stand for me being removed so she pulled me aside and told me to make it look voluntary. She threatened she'd find a way to put me out anyway if I didn't."

Dinah gasped. "When? Where?"

"Monday night. She came into my room and lectured me about the 'dwindling relevance of fan clubs,'" Francine said, making quotation marks in the air with her fingers. "As if the years I've given you meant nothing."

The air in the hallway seemed to thin out. Out of the corner of her eye, Faith saw Chief Garris's hand move toward the set of handcuffs he kept on his belt.

Francine began pacing the hallway. "I couldn't sleep. You'd asked me to show a supportive face, Dinah, but how could I smile and wave as the thing I love was taken from me?"

"Nothing was being taken from you," Dinah said, growing emotion pitching her voice more sharply.

"It's easy for you to say, isn't it?" Francine huffed. "It was bad enough that lots of the things I love about Betty were changing, but to take the Bettys away from me altogether? I knew you'd never have agreed to that. I knew it was all Maura." She stalked up to Ron. "Or him. Even Claudia told me Ron's never liked me."

"That's not what I said," Claudia cut in.

But Francine didn't seem to hear her. "I was up and dressed before dawn. I'm not sure I slept at all. I spent an hour in my room brushing Beatrice because that usually calms me down, but I was still upset. So I left my room and walked around the manor."

Faith watched Francine's face take on the recollection of that morning, the fateful events playing across her expression. She'd come undone, unraveled as completely and irreparably as the sweater Watson had torn to pieces.

"When I saw light through the library door, I thought being in that beautiful, peaceful place among all those lovely books might help me calm down. The door was unlocked. But no, Maura was in there. Exercising even though there's a gym in the manor. Showing no respect for what a library ought to be."

"You did it," Ron said, trying once again to get past the officer and reach Francine. "You killed her. It was you."

Francine's anger dissolved to a frightened awe. "I didn't mean to. We argued. And even that's not true. I don't think she listened to me. She ignored what I had to say. Looked at me as if I didn't matter.

Pulled away from me when I grabbed her arm and pleaded with her to talk to you, Dinah. To see you'd never want this. But no, she went up on that balcony and sneered down at me like I was useless."

Ron went to move toward her again, but the chief silently motioned for no one to interrupt Francine's grisly monologue.

"I followed her up to the balcony. She turned around and laughed." Francine whirled on the group, as if she needed to make sure everyone heard that detail. "She laughed at me. I lunged at her, and we started fighting. She pulled books off the shelves to hit me with. I wrested them away from her and threw them over the balcony. I didn't mean to push her so hard. She went over the railing backward."

The moment struck everyone in the hallway in varying degrees of shock and horror. Dinah covered her mouth. Anne clung to her mother. Ron's expression went from rage to grief.

"I ran down the stairs. She was on the floor with the books all around her. She was so still," Francine said with a disturbing wonder. "Her eyes staring up into nothing, just like they say in the books."

No one said a word.

"When Dinah let it slip that they'd found long rabbit hairs in her bracelet, I realized I had fur all over me from when I'd brushed Beatrice," Francine went on. "That fur had to be from me, from Beatrice. After all, no one else's fur is as long as my magnificent Beatrice's, right?"

"You had to get rid of it," Faith said. "So you sheared Beatrice because no one would ever suspect you of doing that to her."

Francine nodded. "But I had to do more than just my bunny, or it wouldn't look right. It isn't hard to slip into one or two suites of friends, and I found out when everyone would be out of their rooms."

She turned to Pearl. "I knew her fur would grow back. I was careful with all of them. And it would let you win. If you were still there, were still vice president, you wouldn't let them throw me out, right?"

Dinah walked right up to Francine. "You killed Maura over the fan club? How could you hurt me and the Bettys like this?"

Faith loved the members of the Candle House Book Club, considered all of them family as much as her aunt Eileen was, but to murder someone over it? Francine, whom she had once considered so gracious and elegant, suddenly seemed old, lonely, and bitter. It was as sad as it was surprising.

"I didn't mean to," Francine repeated. "I never meant for it to . . ." All the anger seemed to drain out of her body, and she simply stood there, the sentence hanging unfinished in the air.

Garris cleared his throat and walked over to stand behind Francine. "Francine Nelson, I'm placing you under arrest for the murder of Maura Webber." He continued reading her rights as he handcuffed her.

Officer Tobin, Ron, Garris, and Francine filed down the hallway to descend the stairs.

The rest of the hallway occupants regained their collective breaths. For a long moment, no one said a word.

"It was Francine," Faith said, still trying to wrap her mind around the idea. "She's responsible for everything. The murder, the shearing, the rabbits in the library."

"Well," Dinah said, "not all of it."

18

"What do you mean?" Faith asked, not sure how many more twists she could handle this week.

Dinah walked over to Pearl, her former determination returning to her stance as she did so. "Francine did terrible things, but she didn't let the rabbits loose in the library. Pearl did that."

Murmurs rippled through the group.

Pearl? While it didn't have the same weight as the murder that Francine had just confessed to, it still startled Faith and everyone present.

Pearl backed up against the wall.

"I worked it out last night," Dinah told Pearl. "I wanted to see if you would come clean on your own. But clearly, I've overestimated you."

"How did you move the bunnies?" Faith asked.

"The cookies," Dinah replied.

"The ones delivered from Happy Tails each morning?" one of the Bettys gathered in the hallway asked.

"I put Pearl in charge of delivering them to each rabbit owner," Dinah said. "I didn't think anything of it until I heard her telling a member of the housekeeping staff that she'd 'found' a master key. I used to work in a hotel when I was younger. No one loses a master room key. That'd be a terrible breach of security. But you see, if anyone saw Pearl coming in and out of guest rooms with a large box, she could say she was delivering cookies."

"When in fact she was gathering bunnies to let loose in the library," Faith finished for her.

Pearl's demeanor changed now that she'd been found out. She raised her chin defiantly, seeming almost proud to have been behind such a scheme.

"How did you unlock the library?" Faith asked. "The housekeeping master keys don't work on that door."

"*Betty Townsend and the Lucky Locksmith*," Pearl answered.

When Faith gave Dinah a quizzical look, the author said, a little shamefaced, "In the final chapter, I explain quite clearly how to pick a standard lock on a door."

"You always did do outstanding research," Pearl said.

Dinah stood in the doorway to Francine's room, staring into the space Francine had recently vacated.

Over Dinah's shoulder, Faith could see Francine's suitcases still open on the bed and Beatrice in the corner of her hutch. What would become of the rabbit with Francine headed to prison for murder?

"Francine was at least willing to try and build unity among the Bettys," Dinah said. "That's what made her a true president."

"And a murderer," Pearl said bitterly.

"Did you know?" Faith asked Pearl. If Pearl had known of Francine's crimes and kept the information from the authorities, she'd be guilty of more than letting bunnies loose to damage the library.

"No. But Frannie hadn't been herself all week. I knew something was wrong, but I don't think I ever really thought her capable of murder."

"You sabotaged their beautiful library for a petty grudge against the younger Bettys?" Claudia exclaimed.

Pearl turned to Claudia. "How can you ask that? You know what it's like to watch something you love fall to pieces right in front of you."

Instead of letting Claudia answer, Dinah addressed the group. "I know what it's like to see people I thought I could trust betray me in the worst possible way."

Pearl gave a sharp sniff. "I don't have to stay here and listen to this." With that, she stormed into her own room and slammed the door behind her.

Dinah exhaled. "I will see that Pearl repays you for every penny of the damage she's caused." She put a hand wearily to her forehead as she walked into Francine's room. "I don't know how we'll make everything right, but I'll find a way."

Faith followed her, curious to see if her suspicions as to what had drawn Watson's attention were correct. They were. There, lying in one of Francine's open suitcases and partially hidden by clothing, was a sizable plastic bag of rabbit fur in the colors of the three shorn rabbits. "Watson must have picked up on the scent of all this fur," she said, holding up the bag for Dinah to see. "He was trying to show us he knew where it was."

"He is a most extraordinary cat," Dinah agreed. She walked over to the hutch where Beatrice crouched in one corner. "You're still a most extraordinary rabbit, Beatrice, even robbed of your glorious fur. What are we going to do with you?"

"I know a young lady who's looking to own her first rabbit," Faith said, catching Anne's eye. "After all, she's already proven her skills in keeping Beatrice warm."

"I'd be honored," Anne said. "Will Francine let me?"

"I'll talk to her, and I'm sure she'll agree. I've always said every Betty gets a bunny in the end." With a tender expression, Dinah lifted Beatrice from her hutch and handed her to Anne, who sat down on the bed with the animal cradled in her lap.

The sight of Anne stroking Beatrice and murmuring softly to her gave Faith the first spark of hope that Dinah and her Bettys might truly survive this ordeal.

Claudia sat beside her daughter. Now Faith could see the resemblance between the two. "Pearl was right, you know," Claudia said to Dinah. "I have watched something fall apart that I loved. But I blame Ron and Maura, not you."

"I invited you to come," Dinah reminded her.

"Would you have come if you were in my shoes?" Claudia asked.

"I suppose not. But you were welcome. I thought you knew that."

"I never meant to spy. I was worried for you, for what was

happening. Sending Anne was the only way I could think of to come without actually coming. That was wrong, and I'm sorry I did that to you."

Dinah sank onto the chair in Francine's room. "This whole thing is one huge mess. All I ever wanted to do was share Betty's adventures with readers who loved them as much as I did."

"I know that," Claudia said. "I've always known that." After a pause, she asked, "What will you do?"

It was a long time before Dinah replied, "I don't know."

Claudia folded her hands in her lap. "I'd like to help you figure it out. Please let me."

"I'll help too," Anne said. "All the Bettys will."

Dinah gave them a small smile. "Well, it seems I'm in the market for a new editor and someone to lead my Bettys."

Claudia smiled. "How about an old editor?"

"I don't think I'm a president, but I'd love to help you run an online Betty fan page," Anne offered. "You'll need it when the TV series becomes a big hit. And it's a great way to find new Bettys."

Dinah beamed, and it was like the sun had come out on her face. "It's as good a start as any."

Faith walked into the library, feeling as if she'd lived a whole year in the last three hours. She hadn't expected to find anyone waiting for her, so it was a special joy to see the smiling, supportive faces of Brooke, Midge, and Eileen. They, and Watson, were gathered around one of the library tables, which was set with coffee and carrot cake.

Of course she had lots to do before the bus of Bettys left, but for right now, the warmth of her friends and her cat, Brooke's good coffee, and a slice of sweet carrot cake were exactly what Faith needed.

"I'd never have guessed it was Francine," Brooke said as Faith finished her account of what had transpired upstairs.

"Watson did," Faith replied, glad to have her precious feline curled up in her lap after such a harrowing day. "Evidently he'd been trying to tell me by camping outside Francine's door."

"Maybe you really did narrowly escape a bad haircut," Midge said to the cat with a smile.

"It seems to me Watson's narrowly escaped a lot of close calls," Wolfe remarked as he entered the library.

"Is there any more news?" Faith asked.

"I've just gotten off the phone with Garris. Francine's made a formal confession to Maura's murder, and Ron is on his way to New York to be arraigned for his embezzlement charges. Marlene tells me I need to send the bill for library damages to Pearl."

"All three mysteries solved," Eileen said as she offered a slice of cake to Wolfe. "That's cause for celebration."

Brooke stared down at the orange frosting carrot that decorated each slice. "You know, if I don't see another bunny for a while, I'll be perfectly fine with that."

Watson meowed as if to say he agreed wholeheartedly.

Midge nodded. "I'm with you, Watson. It'll be just fine if my clientele sticks with cats and dogs for a long while too."

"I don't think even Dinah could have dreamed up a more surprising ending," Wolfe said.

"It's sad," Faith said as she sank her fork into the moist cake. "Dinah's lost her publisher, her editor, and a friend. All when her career is in the middle of a huge leap in a new direction."

"There's not enough yarn and bunnies in the world to make all of that okay," Eileen said.

"I'm glad she still has Claudia on her side," Midge said. "So she's really Anne's mom and has been keeping tabs on the event this whole time?"

"And from Snickerdoodles to boot," Eileen added. "Jane told me she's never been an accomplice to espionage before."

Faith thought Jane McGee, the owner of Snickerdoodles, was just the kind of person to get a kick out of that. "We may never hear the end of it."

"So what now for our dear Betty Townsend?" Eileen asked. "I'd hate to think this is the end of her adventures."

"I'm sure it won't be," Faith said truthfully. "Dinah seems like she's made of pretty tough stuff. Think of everything Betty Townsend has overcome. That has to get its start in Dinah somehow, don't you think?"

"Betty's one sharp sleuth," Brooke said.

"So is our Faith," Eileen said, hoisting a coffee mug in a toast.

"We all are," Faith replied.

"And Watson," Brooke said. "He found the phone and the fur that broke the case wide open."

At the sound of his name, Watson perked up.

"Looking to take a bow for your brilliant discoveries, Rumpy?" Faith teased, giving him a well-earned scratch under the chin.

"Let's not forget you were the first one to notice Maura's bracelet with those telltale bunny hairs," Brooke said to Watson.

The cat closed his eyes, clearly pleased at the recognition.

"I'd wager our Watson could give Betty Townsend's rabbits a run for their crime-solving money any day of the week," Wolfe said. "But without a sweater."

Everyone laughed as Watson twitched his tail in obvious agreement.

"Maybe we should write our own mystery novels," Eileen suggested with a grin. "In all that spare time I keep hoping we'll have one day."

"No thanks," Faith said. "I love to read and I treasure all our books, but after this event I'll definitely leave the writing to someone else."

"You could still learn to knit," Eileen said. "Get another scarf or maybe a hat under your belt. I bought the most beautiful angora yarn off one of the Bettys at the rabbit show."

"No rabbit yarn," Faith stage-whispered, covering Watson's ears. "At this rate I might get over all this bunny business by the time Easter comes around."

The jingling of keys announced Marlene's arrival in the library. "Here you all are. I've been searching everywhere for you."

"What can we do for you?" Faith asked.

"There are some officers here who would like to examine the library again," Marlene told Faith. "Brooke, we'll need some tea and goodies sent up to Ms. Harper in her suite. And based on what I heard, we need a new system to keep our housekeeping master keys secure. We still do have an estate to run, ladies, so tell your friends to meet up with you later."

Wolfe turned to meet Marlene's glare. "They did just solve a murder."

"And a shearing," Eileen added.

"And whatever it's called when you let rabbits loose in a library for spite," Midge chimed in.

"So I think we can let them finish their cake and coffee," Wolfe said. "Care to join us?"

Marlene scowled. "Some of us have work to do."

"Come on, Marlene," Wolfe coaxed. "We made it through a crazy week. Have some cake."

Brooke held out a slice to the assistant manager.

Marlene paused, then gave in and accepted the cake. "Maybe a small one."

"Then we'd better hop to it," Brooke said with a broad grin.

Groans echoed in the library from Faith and her friends, but they were soon followed by uproarious laughter.

Learn more about Annie's fiction books at

AnniesFiction.com

We've designed the Annie's Fiction website especially for you!

Access your e-books • Read sample chapters • Manage your account

Choose from one of these great series:

Amish Inn Mysteries

Annie's Attic Mysteries

Annie's Mysteries Unraveled

Annie's Quilted Mysteries

Annie's Secrets of the Quilt

Antique Shop Mysteries

Chocolate Shoppe Mysteries

Creative Woman Mysteries

Hearts of Amish Country

Secrets of the Castleton Manor Library

Victorian Mansion Flower Shop Mysteries

What are you waiting for? Visit us now at **AnniesFiction.com!**

Treat yourself to the delightful decadence of the **Chocolate Shoppe Mysteries**—stories that are sure to keep you on the edge of your seat!

Follow the clues with Jillian Green in the enchanting town of Moss Hollow, Georgia, as she mixes up a batch of mystery and intrigue. After twenty years away, a career detour, and a large helping of heartbreak, she returns to the land of sweet tea and Southern charm to help her grandmother run the family business, The Chocolate Shoppe Bakery. Along the way, Jillian is surprised to find that what she lacks in culinary skill, she more than makes up for in amateur detective work! Jillian and her sweet new friends in the local baking club embark on investigations into the curious events taking place in their hometown, with reminders all the while that family, friendships—and a dash of adventure—are essential ingredients to a full and happy life.

Find out more at AnniesFiction.com!

Victorian Mansion
Flower Shop Mysteries™

S et on sparkling Puget Sound in the cozy
island town of Turtle Cove, Washington,
the stories in this enthralling series are
good old-fashioned whodunits chock-full of
fascinating family secrets, breathtaking scenery,
heartwarming discoveries, and the unbreakable
bonds of female friendships.

If you love the great outdoors, gardens, birds,
flowers, and a good mystery book . . . then you'll
love Annie's *Victorian Mansion Flower Shop Mysteries!*

AnniesFiction.com